Crocodile Tears

A Basil Stark Investigation

by Misha Handman

For Wren, without whom this story would literally not have been written.

"You see, Mr. Stark, I'm being stalked by the Crocodile."

In my time, I have heard a lot of unlikely stories. I have been asked to help uncover the location of goods that an elderly relative absolutely meant to include in their wills, but it just slipped their minds. I have had men and women tell me, with all apparent sincerity, that their spouses are trying to divorce them for no reason at all, and they desperately need my help constructing alibis. I was told that Nazi spies were trying to steal the secret of pixie dust to create flying soldiers, and only I could stop them and save democracy. Just last year, I was told that the Korean war would be over in a matter of months, and I was once asked to locate and arrest a man who could, my client told me, walk through walls.

That one turned out to be half-true. It was a massive chore.

But over the last several years, this is the first time that someone has asked me for zoological assistance, and I can't quite keep the skepticism off of my face. "A crocodile, Mr. Driscoll?" I ask, looking across my desk at my latest would-be client. "Surely that is a job for the Regulators. Island wildlife is rather outside my skillset."

Andrew Driscoll gives me a disbelieving look. As clients go, he's more than a little disappointing; a nervous-looking man with an unruly mop of brown hair, a wrinkled suit, and a pencil-thin mustache. To look at him, he's about my age – late thirties, maybe early forties. Of course, looks can be deceiving; I'm quite a lot older than that. I doubt that he can say the same. "Outside your skillset?" he repeats. "But… but you're Basil Stark."

"That is the name on the door," I agree. "You may notice the line underneath that reads, 'Private Investigator', and not, 'Animal Control'. I'm sorry, but I'm really not sure how I can help you with a crocodile."

Driscoll frowns at me. "Not 'a' crocodile, man. 'The' Crocodile. The greatest monster Everland has ever seen. The creature that devoured Captain Hook himself. And now… it's coming for me."

I'm saved from an immediate answer by the arrival of my new secretary, Holly Blossom, bearing two cups of tea. I nod to her, taking one and sipping it thoughtfully. My first inclination, to point out that there were at least two monsters in the island's history much worse than the fabled Crocodile, seems like bad form, so I settle for, "Thank you, Holly," I say. Driscoll takes the other, but doesn't so much as look at her as he does it.

"Not a problem, Uncle Basil," she says, looking between us. "Crocodile?"

"Thank you, Holly," I say again. Driscoll is nervous enough as it is, he doesn't need a young lady hovering over his shoulder waiting for the gory details, especially one liable to shift unpredictably between honest sympathy and ghoulish curiosity. Holly tilts her head, and then nods and retreats into the kitchen – our office isn't large enough to have two rooms, so it's there or taking a walk. "Mr. Driscoll," I add, "What makes you so sure that the Crocodile is… haunting you? As I understand it, there hasn't been a Crocodile sighting since 1947, and there hasn't been a confirmed one since '38. Thirteen years is a long time for a creature that large."

"The ticking, Mr. Stark." Driscoll shudders. "That horrible ticking sound, waking me in the night. When I go to my window, it's gone, but there are prints in the yard. Monstrous, reptilian footprints."

"I see," I say slowly. "And where do you live, Mr. Driscoll?"

"Down on Greenway Street," he says, clutching his tea. "Near the Hill."

I nod, for lack of something better to do. "And you need me to…?"

"I need a way to get rid of it!" Driscoll says. "Mr. Stark, you're a great detective, but you've been here longer than anyone! They told me you were in Everland when the city was founded, that you served as a pirate in the bad old days. They said that you learned woodcraft from the Piccadilly tribe, and knew James Hook himself."

"All true," I agree blandly, "but as you yourself pointed out less than a minute ago, James Hook was eaten by the Crocodile in the end."

"That was decades ago," Driscoll says desperately. "You must have learned something since then."

I sigh, rubbing my forehead, and look down into my tea. "Are you sure someone isn't having you on?"

"Two people have already been eaten, Mr. Stark," Driscoll says.

I look up sharply at that. "I haven't read anything about that," I say. "The newspapers would be jumping all over a series of animal attacks on the Hill."

"The first attack happened in the woods," Driscoll says. "It was chalked off as a mistake. The second, the company brushed off. Treating it as an accident, in the yards. But I know better, Mr. Stark. I saw Sam's body, and it was savaged. And I heard the ticking clock, and ever since I've heard it almost every night. The Crocodile is coming for me, and I don't have long." He shudders. "The Regulators won't help, not without real proof. Not as long as the company is blocking."

"Alright, let's start at the beginning," I say. "What company?"

"Hawthorne Logging, Mr. Stark. Perhaps you've heard of us."

"I think everyone's heard of you," I agree. Hawthorne Logging is one of the largest businesses on the island of Everland. They employ well over a thousand people, a small but measurable percentage of the island's population, including a number of my friends. Despite their name, they're in charge of all resource acquisition on-island – logging, mining, quarrying, the works – but logging remains their main occupation. And while shipping wood from the mainland is doable, Everland wood is particularly strong and tough – almost magical in its resilience, some people say. Stories claim that furniture and houses built from the stuff adapt themselves to their owners, becoming just a little more comfortable and pleasant. I'm not sure that I believe it, myself, but Hawthorne certainly trades on the reputation.

"And what do you do for Hawthorne?"

"I'm a surveyor," Driscoll explains. "Hawthorne buys development rights to swathes of land, and I look over areas that we're thinking of moving into, chart potential issues, and decide whether they're worth prioritizing, putting on the back-burner, or abandoning entirely. If there are animal populations in the region, we need to decide whether to try negotiating with them or leaving them be, or calling in the Regulators. It's rather complicated work."

"I begin to see," I say. "And this Sam character…"

"Sam Acker," Driscoll says. "Another surveyor, yes."

"Was he your partner?"

"Surveyors typically work in rotating pairs," Driscoll says. "I've worked with Sam in the past, but we weren't precisely partners."

"The recent past?"

"A few months ago, most recently. I used to see him around."

"I see. And the first worker that was killed, was that on one of your sites?"

"No, I don't think so," Driscoll says with a frown. "It might have been on one of Sam's. I'd have to check. But I didn't start being stalked until after he died. I think it caught my scent somehow while it was following him."

"Alright, Mr. Driscoll," I say. "I'll investigate your situation. If the Crocodile is on your trail, I'll figure out why. It can't have a taste of you, unless you've lost a limb you haven't mentioned, so I expect we'll be able to find a way to shake it. But honestly, I still think there's another explanation for this."

"Perhaps so, Mr. Stark, and perhaps not." Driscoll nods. "Your secretary already discussed your rates."

"She did, did she," I say, bracing myself.

"Fifty dollars a day, yes?" Driscoll reaches into his pocket, and pulls out a small roll of bills. "Here. Three days' payment. Can you begin at once?"

"Give me an hour to get my files together. I'll meet you at your home, and get started."

"Thank you, Mr. Stark. Thank you so much." Driscoll shakes my hand like it's going out of style, but I eventually manage to get him disengaged and out the door. Holly slips out of the kitchen as it shuts behind him, scooping up his teacup.

"Fifty dollars?" I ask her.

"You were busy, I made something up," she says with a shrug.

"That is a preposterous amount of money."

"Obviously not, if he paid it without blinking." Holly reaches up to pat me on the shoulder. "You're paying me a salary now, Uncle Basil. You have to keep your expenses in mind."

"Remind me," I say, "which of us is looking after whom?"

"Well, which of us promised Mom to look after the other?"

I spend a moment thinking about Plum Blossom. "So both of us, then."

"I figured. I mean, she told me to take care of you, and I'd have been stunned if she didn't tell you to watch out for her little girl. Do you need a refill on the tea?"

"No, I just need to think for a minute. I assume you were eavesdropping?"

"The correct term," Holly calls from the kitchen, "is taking minutes."

"And what did you think of those minutes?"

"I think that the Crocodile is thirty feet long and made mostly of teeth," Holly says. "Or at least, that's what the elders say. You can't reason with it, you can't beat it in a fight, and there is no way it could get all the way from the coastline to the Hill without getting spotted."

"And," I agree, "the Regulators would be all over it if it did. They were founded specifically to deal with animals coming into town, after all."

"If anyone bothered to mention it to them," Holly points out. "That guy seemed to think that Hawthorne would cover it up."

"If they thought it was a general animal attack, they might," I say, "but it would have to be on a good logging site. And if the deaths started piling up, they'd pack up their stake. No profit in dying employees." I frown. "Of course, faking a Crocodile sighting would be a good way to get a site shut down."

"Who would want that?"

"Take your pick," I say. "Criminals, using it as a smuggler's cove. A gang of tigers who know that the company would chase them out of their terrain, but might not mess with a legend. Even one of the Piccadilly, if the site is sacred. God knows not much else keeps Hawthorne out."

"Hm," Holly frowns. "I'm pretty sure I would have heard if that were happening. Mom keeps an ear to the ground for that kind of threat. Heck, I'm pretty sure you would have heard. The tribe keeps you pretty up to date."

I nod. "It could be a new one, but you're probably right. So – criminals, tigers, actually the crocodile. A jealous co-worker, maybe, although killing several people over jealousy seems unlikely."

"Then why take the case?" Holly frowns. "I mean, it sounds like this is a job for the police."

I shrug. "For fifty dollars a day, I'm willing to look into things. I can always go to the police later, if it turns out to be their affair."

"Or you could try to solve it yourself and get arrested again."

"Lies and calumny," I say, grabbing my hat. "I hardly ever get arrested any more."

"You got arrested last week," Holly points out.

"Yes, but it was an exception."

"And last month, on my first day of work, we were raided by the police."

"But they did not technically arrest us," I point out, ducking out the door before she can reply. By the time she reaches the window, shouting something about her mother having to post bail two months ago, I'm halfway down the street and moving at a brisk pace. I still have time before I have to be at Driscoll's house, and the fresh air will do me well.

It's a lovely morning in the Everland sun, with the usual collection of office workers on lunch, street performers passing the time, and families and pickpockets taking some fresh air. I put my hands in the pockets of my jacket and enjoy the fall air, humming quietly. Across the way, a street preacher is yelling something, and I slow to listen.

"When our cares are abandoned, He will return to us!" the preacher yells. "Mankind brought sin to Neverland! We built our houses, and our factories, we brought our ships to darken the shores of a blessed land! We stole the very name of this place, marking it with our arrogance. Everland! A land of sin and depravity from what was once a place of beauty and innocence!" He looks around, and stabs a finger in the direction of a young mother. "Where are the fairies, I ask? Once, they frolicked in the woodlands, and now they are vanished!"

"I had a fairy in my garage a few months back," a heckler calls out. "Took two weeks for the Regulators to come and get rid of it!"

The preacher ignores her; he's got a good head of steam going, and he's not about to waste it on little things like accuracy. "They are vanished," he repeats at a more insistent shout, glaring about him, "and their remains litter our streets, inhaled by the sinful to grant them a moment's peace."

"Pixie dust isn't actually made from pixies," someone else points out.

"And who is responsible for this abomination?" the preacher shouts. "We can see them on the Hill, looming over us like the temple of Mammon! Their factories belch out smoke and churn out weapons, and they pay for their place with the blood money they harvest from the dreams of the innocent children they've ruined by corrupting this place! They call themselves Second Star, but they are the spawn of Satan himself! Do not trust them, my friends! Turn your face away from their lies! Return this island to what it once was! Let the children frolic once again! Bring back the Pan!"

I've heard enough. "Frolic?" I say. "This place was a graveyard. Dozens of Lost Boys murdered, by every manner of monster."

The preacher's eyes fix on me. "This was a beautiful land," he snarls.

"Beautiful, yes," I agree. "But deadly. Ask the Police Commissioner what he thinks of returning to those days, if you feel like resting a night on the city's dime. He was one of the Lost Boys you think so highly of, after all, before he escaped."

The preacher snorts. "What would you know of the Pure Times?" he asks, looking me up and down. "You're no Lost Boy."

"No," I say, taking a step forwards. "I was a pirate."

The crowd goes quiet, looking between us. The preacher is looking uncertain now. "The pirates all died," he says, "all except for…" He blanches.

"All except for Gentleman Starkey?" I ask quietly. "Captain Hook's first mate, and the only man living who fought the Pan?" I stare at him. "Bring him back?" I repeat. "You have no idea what you're asking for. This place is better off without him, wherever he went."

The preacher starts to bristle, but he looks around and sees that the crowd isn't about to step in. "Heretic," he snarls, backing very quickly away from me. "Of course you wouldn't mourn for what was lost!"

"No one here mourns what was lost," I say. "You're preaching to the wrong crowd. Get out of here."

The preacher looks like he wants to press the point, but it's clear that words are his weapon, and he seems to have a good idea about what would happen if he tries to make things physical. He manages to turn his retreat into a dignified one, continuing to shout about my sins, but his heart isn't in it, and the crowd quickly starts to disperse. I shake my head.

"Damned Pannites," I mutter. "I thought they'd stopped preaching after Darling threatened to have the whole congregation arrested."

"They're riled up, the last few days," a businessman says. "I heard a rumour that the Crocodile's about. Got them thinking their saviour's coming back."

"Ridiculous," I mutter. "The Crocodile didn't even work with him."

The man laughs. "That's cults for you." He pauses. "Are you really him? The pirate fellow?"

"Not for a long time," I say, walking away with a tip of my hat.

I make my way to Driscoll's house without any further interruptions, and find him sitting on his porch, nervously smoking a pipe and watching the street for me. "I thought you'd be here sooner," he says.

I pull out my pocket watch and glance at it. "Sorry. I did say an hour, though. It's only been forty-five minutes."

"Has it?" Driscoll winces. "I don't have my pocket watch on me right now. The ticking, you see. Thought it had been longer."

I frown. He really is a mess. "Why don't you show me to those crocodile tracks, and we'll see about getting to the bottom of this."

He leads me around the side of the house. It's one of the 1930s models that was built in droves during the Depression, when the city really started to take shape – a mix of brick and local wood, fairly large but not extravagant. With its lawn and actual picket fence, it's nearly identical to every other house in the neighborhood. Mr. Driscoll's one nod to individuality is a coat of light green paint; otherwise, he's toeing the neighborhood line. He even has the three flags flying over his front door – American, British, and Everland's two stars flanking a golden sun. The side of the house contains a garden bed, filled mainly with rose bushes.

"This is where I found the marks," Driscoll says, leading me to a bush that has seen better days. I have to admit, if I were to imagine what a rose bush might look like after a thirty-foot crocodile leaned on it, it would be a lot like this. The ground is churned up, and while I can't make out clear prints, there are definite suggestions of claws. "I heard the ticking first, last night, and then a huge crash. I turned on the lights, and went for my rifle, but when I got to the window there was nothing there."

"Nothing?" I say. "I can't imagine how it could have gotten away that quickly." I look around. "Not much cover around here. A few hedges, large enough to conceal a person or a small tiger, perhaps, but not the Crocodile. No broken sewer grates, either."

"I'm telling you, it was here."

"Something was." I kneel by the garden, inspecting the ground, and draw lines with my mind. "Damned polite for a Crocodile, though."

"Sorry?"

I gesture back towards the street. "Well, whatever came in either vaulted your fence, or used the gate. No churned up grass, and your fence is intact, so a giant

Crocodile didn't barrel through it, and the thing can't exactly jump. Which makes him surprisingly thoughtful, using the gate that way."

"Are you making fun of me, Mr. Stark?"

"Sorry. That wasn't the intent."

"Then what, precisely, *was* the intent?"

"I'm a detective, Mr. Driscoll, I'm pointing out a problem with the theory we have so far. If the Crocodile was at your window, how did it get into the yard? Never mind getting down the street."

"If it wasn't," Driscoll says, "what killed Sam and that logger?"

"That's a wonderful question," I agree. "I think, if we want to find an answer, we're going to have to go to the source. I'd like to visit Hawthorne Logging, if you don't mind."

For a moment, it looks as though Driscoll minds very much, and I'm half-convinced he's going to demand I leave his workplace alone. But then he sighs, and nods. "You can stop by this evening. I was just about to head in, anyway."

"Odd hours."

"Half the office is shut down until the loggers and survey teams start coming in. So whenever we have office work to do, we do it in the afternoon and evening." Driscoll glances to the crushed rose bushes, and back to me. "I used to like heading home after dark. You had the whole world to yourself."

"As a night owl myself, I know the feeling. Right. I'll do some poking around, see if there have been any other Crocodile sightings in the area, and come down to meet you." I pause. "I assume you want my inquiries to be discreet?"

"What I want, Mr. Stark, is not to find myself on the inside of a beast. Whatever you must do, you must, but, please do it quietly. I don't want to be the laughingstock of the company."

"Of course, Mr. Driscoll," I say, tipping my hat to him. "I'm the soul of discretion."

I spend the next couple of hours as I promised, running down rumours. To my surprise, there actually are some. A Piccadilly logger is taking a few days off because some of his mates heard ticking in the woods, and he knows well enough what that means. I get the location from him, and add it to my list. A reporter that owes a few small favors to me lets me know that there was a Hawthorne logger killed, one Jim Thatch, but that the company called it an accident. Given how many lumberjacks die every year, there didn't seem to be a need to dig further. I suggest to her that there may be a story in it, and promise to give her the details if they won't jeopardize my client. I also stop by the library, and pull the papers for Crocodile stories from the last thirty years.

The stories don't surprise me. The Crocodile has been seen on and off in Everland since colonization. The first sighting was almost immediately after landfall, when it took out a half-dozen workers building Second Star's first facilities. Throughout the 1920s, it popped up every few weeks, always on the edges of the city. Sometimes it would attack someone, sometimes it was only spotted. Occasionally it would let a victim go, but usually survivors were attacked again in the next few weeks, until they either fled the island or died. By the 1930s, though, the Crocodile was either getting cautious, or old. Stories and clippings started to fall off, and confirmed kills dropped dramatically. There was a rumor in 1938 that the Regulators had managed to corner and kill the creature, although they never provided a body. After that, there were no confirmed incidents, only suspected ones. In the end, one crocodile attack looks a lot like another, and the island has never had any shortage of cunning, deadly animals.

Thusly armed with a lot of stories and very few facts, I flag down a taxi and take it up to the Hawthorne Company's lumber yard, conveniently located on the absolute outskirts of town, nearby to nothing and no one. The lumber yard is busy; a veritable forest of stacked timber on one side of the yard, with more arriving on horse-pulled sleds. On the other side of the vast lot, stacks and stacks of freshly-cut lumber are ready to be taken by truck down to the docks, and from there to be shipped to luxury construction sites around the world.

The guard at the front gate watches me suspiciously, and doesn't seem any calmer when I tell him I'm here to see Driscoll. Once he gets the okay, though, he waves me through, directing me to the main building and telling me not to wander around. I choose to listen to him, for the moment. No sense getting thrown out before I know what I'm looking for. Driscoll himself is waiting for me at the main doors, hands in his pockets and glancing nervously around. "Mr. Stark," he says, nodding to me. "No trouble getting here, I hope?"

"None at all, Mr. Driscoll. Why don't you show me around? Afterwards, I can do a bit of poking on my own."

"Alright, but again, I don't really see how this is helpful." Driscoll leads me into the main offices, heading up the stairs to the second floor. "I mostly work in the surveying department, of course. There are eight surveyors, plus a couple of supervisors who spend their time here at the office, and we pair off more or less randomly depending on who's free when a new sector needs to be looked at."

"Driscoll!" The bellow comes from across the room, and the two of us look over in time to see a pale, burly man in an ill-fitting suit storming towards us. An incongruous pair of spectacles are perched carefully on his nose, and he glares over them at my client. "Where the hell have you been? And who the hell is this?"

"Oh! Mr. Ellis, hello, I'm sorry," Driscoll babbles. "This is my… friend, Basil, he's, uh, working with me on a, um, well, he's sort of a local expert..."

"I don't care if he's a local genius!" Mr. Ellis roars. "I've been trying to get in touch with you for the last half-hour!"

Heads are turning in the office, and Driscoll winces. "Mr. Ellis, please, volume, sir. Mr. Stark, that is, Basil, this is Ralph Ellis, he's the evening shift supervisor for the surveying department."

"Damn it, Driscoll, get rid of him and get into my office! Did Ms. Wescoff get a hold of you?"

"Ms. Wescoff?" Driscoll's brow furrows, as Ellis grabs him by the shoulder and ushers him into a side office. "I don't think I know…" His voice is cut off as the door slams, leaving me more or less standing on my own.

"Well," I say, to no one in particular.

"Oh, don't mind Ralph, he's a sweetheart, really. Panics easy, I suppose." I turn to find a hand extended. "Kathryn Zhang. I partner up with Andrew pretty often. I don't believe he's ever mentioned you, Mr… Stark, was it?"

I shake her hand. "It was," I agree, sizing her up. Probably Chinese, mid-thirties, dressed much like I would expect from a surveyor in the office – sensible shoes, hiking pants, a blouse for form's sake and short-cut hair. Firm handshake, too, or at least firmer than Driscoll's. "Basil Stark. A pleasure to meet you, Ms. Zhang. What was all that about, if you don't mind my asking?"

"Oh, I don't know," she says airily, waving it off. "One of the engineers has some issue with a report, and she's tearing around bothering everyone. Happens all the time. Not one of mine, I don't think, but we've all been pulling extra duty since poor Sam…" She breaks off. "I suppose you heard about that from Andrew?"

"Sam Acker, the surveyor?" I nod. "Andrew mentioned that there was an accident of some kind."

"Accident, my left foot. Damned fool went out on a survey without his partner, and got himself eaten. We've roped the area off, of course."

"Not calling the Regulators?" I ask innocently. Ms. Zhang laughs.

"Basil – can I call you Basil?" I nod, and she pushes on. "Basil, we don't call the Regulators for incidents in the woods. There are animals in the woods. That's not exactly a surprise, and it's not a safety issue. The Regulators only step in if the animals come into town, or if something magical comes our way. A bear attack is neither."

"So it was a bear?" I ask.

"I'm sure I don't know what it was. I'm a surveyor, not an animal expert." She sizes me up again. "And what do you do? I don't suppose you're an animal expert?"

"I'm just a meddlesome guy," I say with a smile, walking over to look over the survey map pinned to the wall. There's a patchwork of green, blue, and red zones covering it, along with a handful of yellow squares. "Quite the extensive operations."

"Aren't they just? The yellow spots are our current logging camps. Green areas are where they're logging, and blue are in the process of surveying. Red, of course, are roped off. Too dangerous, or not profitable enough, or just too much opposition to logging."

"I'm surprised that opposition matters."

Ms. Zhang laughs again, although this time there's a definite edge to it. "There's plenty of island, Basil, and we're the only company managing it. No sense looking for trouble."

I glance over the red zones, noting that each one has a pair of names and a date attached to it. "I can't help but notice that there are three of those dangerous spots quite close to one another."

"Hm? Oh, yes, that happens."

"I also notice that some of them have two names, and some have four."

"Two names are for dangerous areas – anywhere that an incident happens," Kathryn explains, stepping up to gesture at the map. "Four indicates that the cost of logging wouldn't be worth the return; we have a second team of surveyors come in to confirm in those situations."

"Right. So this one," I tap one red zone lightly, "would be where that logger died. Mr. Thatch, I think it was."

"Yes, poor soul," Zhang says, the warmth leeching out of her voice.

"And... oh, dear, I see that Sam Acker was the one who signed off on that, along with you. I'm sorry, I didn't mean to bring up recent pains." I frown, looking at the map. "And then he went out to the next zone over, by himself. Odd."

"Tragic, I would say." Zhang's voice is frosty. "Sam was a sensitive soul. He was quite torn up about Mr. Thatch, I assume he went out to look around because he was worried that another accident might happen."

"And it did," I say evenly.

"And it did," Zhang agrees. "Where exactly did you say you worked, Mr. Stark?"

I'm still looking at the map. "And this site, not too far away. Grid 14-H. Another accident? No, wait, I see that there are four names, not two. Unfit for logging, then." I pause. "Signed by Andrew, along with a Mr. Collins. And you and poor Mr. Acker confirmed the findings. What an odd coincidence." I look over, and Zhang is glaring daggers at me. "Oh, dear, am I being indecorous, Ms. Zhang? I am so sorry."

"What the devil is going on over here?" I look over, to see what I presume is another of Driscoll's co-workers walking up – he has matching boots and pants to Ms. Zhang, although he seems to have chosen a light jacket rather than her blouse. He's also rather shorter than she is, and he glares up at the pair of us. "You're not a surveyor," he tells me.

"Perceptive of you," I agree. "I suppose it was the coat that gave me away."

"Day labourers aren't allowed up here," the man says. "Get back to your sled."

"Now, Jake," Ms. Zhang interrupts. "This is Basil Stark. A friend of Andrew's."

If Jake looked angry before, he's closer to apoplectic now. "I've never heard of him."

"Nevertheless, that seems to be my role in all of this," I say, holding out my hand. "And you are…"

"I don't care if you're a friend of John Darling himself, you're not allowed up here!" Jake ignores my hand, steps in front of the survey map, and makes vague shooing motions. "You can wait for your 'friend' outside, like everyone else!"

"Well. It was a pleasure to meet you, Mr. Collins. Would you let Andrew know that I'll be back in a few hours."

"It wasn't a pleasure to meet you," he snaps back. I smile slightly, and nod to both him and Ms. Zhang. He looks furious, she looks concerned, and I don't blame her. It was a shot in the dark, but Mr. Collins seems to have confirmed it for me rather nicely. Either he didn't notice me guess his name, or he assumed that Driscoll had already given it to me.

As I stroll down the stairs, I consider what I've learned, if anything. It's already obvious that Driscoll is holding something back, probably something that will actually resolve this case, and almost certainly related to that mysterious patch of forest. Four surveyors listed it as being not worth developing, despite being, relatively speaking, right next to the company's western logging camp. One of them is dead, one of them thinks a crocodile is hunting him, and the other two are inordinately interested in the visitor he brought to the office. No one else seemed to notice me poking around, or at least weren't willing to mention it.

I could grill Driscoll, but I decide I might as well take a look myself. It's been a few years since I've done much hiking, but there are sleds coming and going all over the place. I head over to a lumberjack who looks familiar, and nod to him. "Afternoon, Gordon."

"Well, I'll be. Basil Stark!" Gordon grins, and pumps my hand enthusiastically. "What brings you all the way out here? I haven't seen you since that business with the shadow actors!"

"Oh, just following up on a case. Probably nothing too serious, but I was wondering – would you happen to be heading up to the western logging camp any time soon?"

"Nah, I'm assigned to the east." Gordon considers. "Oh, but there's someone might be willing to take you, if you don't mind a little detour."

"A little detour?"

"Yeah, there's some engineer doing research up that ways. Amos was going up to pick her up in a few minutes, and you can probably hitch a ride with him, no problem."

There can't be that many women engineers at the logging camp. I take a deep breath. "He wasn't swinging past Grid 14-H by any chance?"

"Might be," Gordon answers uncertainly. "Didn't really ask."

"Maybe I should take you up on that. Point Amos out to me, and I'll take my chances on that detour."

Amos, as it turns out, is a good friend of Gordon's, and unfortunately also something of an admirer of mine. I've barely managed to get my name out before he's offering me a place in his Jeep in place of the logger he was planning to drag along to act as his partner. While he checks the Jeep over he throws a non-stop barrage of questions my way; I've felt less under siege in actual sieges. But soon enough, the two of us are on our way, heading into the mountains. "Nice car," I say, patting the side. "War surplus?"

Amos nods, with a grin. "Hawthorne picked up a whole set of 'em. Great for Everland forests. We have to use horses for the logs, of course – can't fit a big truck in the forests – but these cars are a lot faster for sending messages and the like."

"So, this engineer we're picking up – Ms. Wescoff, was it?"

"That's her. Nice dame, a bit pushy sometimes, but that's an engineer for you, right?" Amos chuckles. "Goes with the job."

"What's she doing out in the woods alone?"

"Oh, she's not alone," Amos says with a laugh. "You don't go out in the woods alone. No, she's got a logger with her." He nods. "Yeah, she thought the surveyors who looked over that grid didn't do a great job. Thought there should be metals there, or some such. You know we do a bit of mining, sometimes? I mean, not me personally, of course. But…"

"Yeah," I nod. Everland still has places where metal's right up at the surface. Easy enough for Hawthorne to set up a few open pits after they clear out the trees, get twice as much work done in a single site. "That would make it worth developing, I guess?"

"Hell yeah, it would. I mean, depending on how much ore were there. Ms. Wescoff thought the surveyors didn't know what to look for, maybe. Raised a stink, and went out herself when the supervisor tried to make her wait for them to get back." He pauses. "You heard about the guy who got ate, I guess."

"I heard."

"Well, he was the guy who looked the place over the first time, so she couldn't check with him, and his partner wasn't around, so she went up on her own. Supervisor damned near passed out, he was yelling so loud, but he's not her boss so what's he gonna do." He looks over at me. "Say, what are you doing up in the mountains?"

"At this point, I'm a little curious to meet Ms. Wescoff," I say. "But I'm actually involved in something else. Did you know Jim Thatch?"

"Poor guy. Sure, I knew him. Logging camps aren't so big that you don't meet the other lumberjacks, and you're out there day and night, facing trees and fairies and lions and whatnot, you get to know 'em pretty fast." He nods grimly. "They should'ave called the Regulators in, when he died. Weren't no normal animal attack. Jim, he took his precautions. Carried a horn, knew how to be careful. Knew how to climb a tree." He shakes his head. "If it had been tigers… maybe. Tigers are smart, they climb, and they're mean. Once knew a tiger that tried to convince me it was another logger, stuck in a hedge. Kept yelling for me to come in after it. I fired my gun as a warning, damn thing exploded out of the hedge and near took off my leg before I got it. But you can tell a tiger kill, and anyway, they don't hang around the western side of the island."

"What do you think killed him, then?" I ask. "Human?"

"Not unless you know a human can bite a man in half without breaking a sweat. They found what was left down by the river. Wasn't there, but the stories I heard was bad enough. It were a croc, and a damned big one."

"You think it was **the** Croc?"

Amos considers. "Could be. Hard to say. There are some damned big crocs on this island. Don't rightly know the difference between huge and monstrous. But it weren't a normal one."

After that, we drive in silence for a few minutes, lost in our respective thoughts. When the conversation resumes, we silently agree to move to lighter topics, discussing friends we both know, some of my more comical old cases, and Amos's troubles with his girlfriend. It's a good hour of rolling through wooded pathways, as the sun slowly lowers above the treeline. By the time we reach the edge of the sector where our engineer is, the shadows are getting long, and Amos, for all his laughter, is looking a little bit nervous.

Looking over Grid 14-H, I'm inclined to agree with the surveyors. The land out here is near a set of bluffs and rolling hills leading to a cliff overlooking the Sea of Dreams. The waves are crashing against the rocks, and the clouds roil in the distance, obscuring the horizon. There are no ships on the water, not on this side of the island – there's nothing for them to sail to. It's picturesque, but the trees are scraggly little things, surrounded by heavy brush and thick grasses. We climb out of the Jeep, and take a look around. "Should we bellow for her?" I ask.

"She should be back here already," Amos says with a frown. He raises his voice and yells out over the hills. "Betty? You around here?"

"Over here," comes the call from down the hill. Amos and I share a look.

"Engineers," he mutters. "Wouldn't know to make a pick-up time if their lives depended on it."

The two of us push through the brush land, cresting a hill to find what is presumably Ms. Wescoff and her companion. She is kneeling in what looks like churned-up mud, turning over a piece of something in one hand. She looks up, brushes a strand of black hair that's come loose from a ragged ponytail out of one eye, and smiles. "Oh, hello, Amos. I thought you weren't coming until five."

"It's 5:30, Betty," Amos says, trying not to smile.

"Knew it," the other man mutters. He nods to us. "Jeep back up the hill? Betty, I'm going to wait there. Finish with your rocks, and come on."

Betty Wescoff chuckles. "You'll have to forgive Simon," she says to us. "He thinks this whole operation is a waste of time?"

I kneel down beside her, looking at the mud on the ground. "And was it?"

"Hard to say," Ms. Wescoff idly turns the object she's holding over in her hands. Up close, it looks like a chunk of badly-formed metal, about the size of a lumpy golf ball. "There's definitely some metal here, but the surveyors might have been right. Not enough to really set up a mine, especially given that we couldn't clear the brush for lumber. This areas seems to be prone to forest fires – no old growth trees."

"But?"

"Look at the mud here, and here," Ms. Wescoff says, gesturing. I step up beside her, and nod slowly.

"Tire tracks."

"Lots of them. I'd say there were Jeeps out here, and a lot of them."

"Tourists?"

Ms. Wescoff gives me a disbelieving look. "Out here? There's nothing interesting for miles."

"Oh, I don't know," I say mildly, gesturing to the cliff. "It's a nice view."

There's a short pause. "You're teasing," she finally says.

"Oh, thank God, someone noticed. Everyone seems to think I'm a serious man for some reason." I hold out my hand. "Basil Stark."

"Oh! I'm sorry, I was so busy with the work... Betty Wescoff. Call me Betty. I'm one of the head engineers at Hawthorne Lumber, not that they need many of us." Betty frowns thoughtfully. "You don't look much like a lumberjack, Basil."

Amos jumps in. "Mr. Stark is a detective, Betty. He's looking into what happened to Jim Thatch."

"Oh, that poor man," Betty says. "What are you doing all the way out here?"

"Youthful curiousity," I say with a grin. "What is that you're holding?"

"Oh, this? I found it under a bush." Betty brandishes it. "Iron, I think. Possibly meteoric. See the serrations? It broke off of a larger fragment. I was wondering if I might find that one somewhere around here. A small starstrike could explain the forest fires, and why the metal index is off. But instead, I just came across the tire tracks."

"It sounds like someone stole your find," I say, looking more closely at the iron. "May I see that for a moment?"

"I wouldn't call it stealing," Betty says, passing it over. "It's…" She breaks off. "Did you hear something just now?"

I hesitate. Amos is looking between us, and for a moment all I can hear is breathing. And then…

Tick tock. Tick tock.

"Oh dear," I whisper. "Betty, Amos, I think we should move for the Jeep. Quickly. But very quietly, do you understand?"

"What is it?" Betty asks, lowering her voice to match mine. "It sounds like…"

There's a cry of fear from up the hill. I swear under my breath and break into a run, Amos and Betty a few steps behind me. And as we crest the hill, we see the Crocodile.

Mere description doesn't do the thing justice. I don't think it's actually thirty feet long, probably only about twenty-five, which to be fair is still by far the largest creature around. Its jaws are just a little too large, its legs just a little too long. The skin, such a dark green it's almost black, with rainbow hints in the setting sunlight, is straight out of old forgotten nightmares. The monster is advancing on Simon, who is cowering in the Jeep. It has the vehicle almost completely surrounded, and its mouth is opening. We're only a few moments away from another dead logger.

"Your rifle?" I ask Amos. Wordlessly, ashen-faced, he points to the shattered remains lying in front of the Jeep. It looks like Simon already tried that.

There's really only one chance. Without thinking I break into a sprint, moving away from the Jeep and the others at a dead run. I take the hunk of metal I took from Betty, wind up, and throw it as hard as I can at the monster's head. My aim isn't quite dead on – I was hoping for the eye, but I end up scraping the top of its ridge. It's enough to get its attention, though. With a bellow of rage, it pauses just long enough to snap at the metal, swallowing it whole, before uncoiling from the Jeep and coming after me.

"Get in the Jeep!" I shout, racing for the cliff, pursued by two tonnes of angry Crocodile. "I'll be right back!"

The good news is, giant crocodiles aren't much faster than regular-sized ones, and this is not ideal crocodile territory. The bad news is, this crocodile seems to have more stamina than the regular sort. I'm outpacing him for the moment, but a glance over my shoulder shows him slowly but steadily gaining on me, and while I wouldn't call myself a scholar of reptilian faces, he definitely looks angry. Or hungry. Or both.

I have a plan, but it's increasingly looking like a terrible one. We're racing downhill now, the monster gaining on me with every second. The bushes and briars are slowing me down, forcing me to take precious half-seconds to leap over or turn aside from difficult ground, whereas the crocodile is just smashing straight through, leaving a trail of devastation in his wake. He's no more than twenty feet away from me, and when I look over my shoulder again all that I can see are jaws and a thrashing tail filling my vision. I decide that it's a good time to return my attention to what's in front of me, just in time to narrowly avoid a gorse bush. I stumble, changing my direction slightly, and the bush explodes into splinters as the Crocodile plows through it. He is definitely gaining on me.

And then the ground ahead is falling away abruptly, and I change my direction entirely, feet scrabbling for purchase on the rocks as I shift ninety degrees while still trying to maintain total forward momentum. I feel breath on my back, and then the Crocodile, who attempts the same maneuver, fails it completely, legs flailing as it turns, skidding in its original direction. The cliff side isn't quite up to handling its weight, and rock and dirt falls away from the edge as I throw myself forwards. For a moment, I'm staring the beast in the eyes, only a few feet between us.

Tick.

And then it's over the edge, before the clock can sound again, falling down towards the sharp rocks below. I scramble back to solid ground, heart pounding in my chest, staring at the cliff. Of course, the Crocodile isn't about to climb back up. Of course. In just a few more minutes, I think I'll actually start to believe that.

I hear the sound of feet racing down the hill, and look to see Betty Wescoff brandishing a rifle, swinging it wildly back and forth. Amos and Simon are coming more cautiously, sticking a little bit too close to one another, eyes wild. "Where did it go?" Betty yells, waving the rifle in my direction.

I point over the edge, panting heavily. "It's gone. For now. Please put that thing away before I take a bullet."

"What? I... oh." Looking abashed, Betty lowers the rifle and approaches the edge of the cliff. "Is it dead?"

"I doubt a little thing like a hundred-foot fall onto sharp rocks could stop it," I say, shaking my head. "It's probably swum off, to find a way back up here. I suggest we be gone when it arrives." And then realization hits. "Hold on, didn't I tell you all to wait at the Jeep?"

"We tried, Mr. Stark, honest," Amos says, wringing his hands. "She wouldn't hear of it. Grabbed the spare rifle, loaded it fast as you like, and came running after you."

"It took me a little less time." Betty gestures back the way I came from, at the smashed-flat trail the Crocodile had left in its wake. "What was it doing here?"

"I have a theory," I say, letting Amos help me back to my feet. I check my coat – a few minor tears from the brush, but nothing serious. "I'll tell you about it while we're getting the hell out of here."

We return to the Jeep, which has some long claws marks in its door, but fortunately hadn't taken the brunt of the Crocodile's attack. Amos starts the engine, and we take off at all speed. "Simon," I ask, "did you by chance also find a small chunk of metal? I'm afraid that I lost Ms. Wescoff's." In the front seat, Betty snorts, sounding faintly hysterical.

"Uh, yeah, sure," Simon says, digging through his pockets. He looks worse than Betty, and I don't blame him, but the conversation seems to be calming him down a bit. "Thought it might make a neat souvenir, and Ms. Wescoff already had hers." He comes up with a much smaller piece than Betty's – no larger than a couple of marbles crushed together. "That's okay, right?"

"It's what the Crocodile was after," I say. "You noticed it stopped to eat the one I tossed its way?"

"I did not," Simon says. "I only noticed I was about to die, and then there you were."

"I noticed," Betty says. "I thought it was just angry."

"More than angry. It wanted those fragments." I turn the piece over, studying it closely, and nod slowly. "I thought so."

"What did you think?" Betty ask.

"That I need to have a long conversation with someone," I say, pocketing the marble. "Mind if I hang on to this for a little while?"

"If that monster can smell it, you can hang on to it forever," Simon says earnestly.

"Now hang on just one minute," Betty says. "What would a crocodile want with a lump of iron?"

"Not just any lump of iron," I say. "Not even just normal meteoric iron. Your theory was right. This is starstone."

"So it was a starstrike that started that fire," Betty says slowly. "I didn't know the Crocodile was interested in dead stars."

"Neither did I, but it has to keep its magic somehow. They say the stars know all the paths of the Sea of Dreams, after all. Maybe that's how it sneaks around so well."

"That's just a myth, though," Betty says. "Starstone has some strange properties, yes – you can't reach Everland without a starfinder compass. But it's not alive."

"We just faced off against a thirty-foot long ticking crocodile. The line between truth and myth gets more than a little blurred out here."

Betty subsides, frowning thoughtfully, and Amos says, "Who do you need to talk to?"

"My client," I say grimly.

Driscoll nervously adjusts his tie, looking around the room. "I'm not sure what you mean, Mr. Stark," he says. "I told you everything about the case. And now that you've seen the Crocodile, you must agree that it's after us."

Our return to Hawthorne's main offices created a lot of noise. Even if I'd been inclined to cover up the Crocodile's appearance, which I wasn't particularly, none of my companions wasted any time telling everyone within earshot what had happened. Amos and Simon had wandered off in search of several stiff drinks, and Betty Wescoff had marched straight up to management to get the entire Western logging camp shut down for the time being, until we could confirm that the Crocodile had moved on. I wasn't sure about her chances, but at least she was trying. Rumours flew around all three of their paths, and by the time I cornered Driscoll in the cafeteria, he'd already heard several (likely inaccurate) stories of my battle with the monster. I'd taken advantage of his obvious terror to drag him into a side office for interrogation, which was going about as well as I'd expected.

"You didn't mention the scheme you'd cooked up with Sam Acker, for a start," I say pointedly. "Or should I say the scheme you cooked up with Acker, Zhang and Collins?" Driscoll gives a start, and I reach into my pocket, pulling out the lump of starstone we recovered at the site. "Does this look at all familiar to you?"

Driscoll swallows. "I don't think…" he starts.

"Right, then. I think this concludes my investigation, Mr. Driscoll. Stop by the office tomorrow, and I will have Holly refund you the next two days' pay." I stand firmly, pocketing the starstone again. "Give my regards to the Crocodile."

"Wait, wait!" Driscoll surges to his feet, grabbing for my coat. "You're right! Just… just sit down. Just don't let it get me."

I rub my forehead. "I don't much like it when I have to investigate my clients, Mr. Driscoll."

"I know. But it wasn't my secret to give! If I told you, the others would have exploded." Driscoll sighs heavily. "They all still thought I was making it all up, or at least imagining it. I bet they don't think that now."

"If I'm going to work for you, I want the whole story. I have a pretty good idea, but I want the details."

"There were five of us, not four. It all started when Jake and I were out surveying the western grid. You were down there, I think? It was useless for logging, of course, but that hardly mattered. Not with what we found."

"Which was?"

"A celestial graveyard, Mr. Stark. Full and intact."

My breath catches in my throat. "How many stars?"

"Thousands, most of them undamaged. Well over two million dollars' worth of material, just lying on the ground." Driscoll shakes his head. "It was the find of a lifetime. It's been years since anyone stumbled across an entire graveyard. I've heard rumours that the stars weren't falling to Everland anymore."

"Probably true. Not safe for them here. Too many people cutting up their corpses for science." I lean back in my chair. "I assume Hawthorne offers a commission for discovering things like that."

"Yes, five percent on anything classified as a treasure, rather than a resource. Of course, since legally Second Star has claim to any starstone found on-island the rates are fixed, and rather lower than market value. Still, it probably would have worked out to around fifteen thousand dollars each for us, quite a tidy sum. We couldn't stop talking about it. We agreed to keep quiet, until we got back to speak with Ralph. We didn't want loggers swarming the site to try and take a piece home with them."

"Ralph. Your panicking supervisor?"

Driscoll winces. "Yes. Jake and I reported the find, and outlined how large we expected it to be. We assumed he would call up Hawthorne and get some security to the find. Ralph had a better idea, or so he told us. He had connections. People overseas willing to pay for celestial iron, for their own research. People who would pay a good deal above market rates for quiet delivery, and the proceeds could be divided up among us. He offered us three hundred thousand dollars each to be part of the scheme, Mr. Stark. He dangled the money in front of our eyes, talked it up until it seemed the most reasonable thing in the world. It was a victimless crime, after all. The starstone wasn't Hawthorne property yet, so it wasn't as though we were really stealing from the company, and no one has much love for Second Star around here. If they don't get some starstone they never knew was here, well. It would be easy to categorize the site as useless, then spend a week moving it off-site ten or twenty stones at a time. They could be hidden in the survey Jeeps, smuggled back into town, and prepared for transport. Ralph's contacts would pay us for the shipments, and we would all be able to retire rich. There was only one problem."

"Surveyors sign off on useless sites."

"Exactly. Which is where Kathryn and Sam entered this sordid little story." Driscoll rubs his forehead. "I don't know exactly why Ralph chose them. I think he might have done something like this with them before, if on a much, much smaller scale. For whatever reason, he told us he could talk them into it, promised to keep our names out of it until they were committed. For equal shares, of course. After all, if we were all sharing in the risk, we should all share in the reward. Six shares total – one for each surveyor, one for Ralph, and one for his contact. It all seemed fair enough to me. Three hundred thousand dollars is enough money for me to live on for the rest of my life. I thought perhaps I would move away, set up a new life in America and claim to have inherited the money from a British relation. Work part-time, and live a comfortable life."

"Not a bad plan," I agree. "On paper."

"You don't think it was… wrong?" Driscoll asks.

I breathe out slowly. "Well, as crimes go, it has the advantage of being bloodless, and you're right – while you're technically defrauding both Hawthorne and Second Star, you aren't taking anything they have. Personally, I think only giving a five percent finders' fee is extortion. Hawthorne is practically begging for you to steal from them." I shake my head. "On the other hand, it was full of dumb moments, the first of which was… well, I'm guessing selling the rocks hasn't been quite so easy."

"No," Driscoll says with a sigh. "We hid the starstone successfully, and then divided it into five shipments to move into town. Ralph got the first shipment off, no problem, but the payout wasn't quite what we expected. It should have been about sixty thousand each, and instead it was about forty. Ralph said it was because of bribes to smuggle the rocks out, and the next shipment would cost less. But then… well, then the logger died. Thatch. As soon as that happened, Hawthorne had investigators down, and we all had to duck and cover. We didn't have anything to do with it, but we couldn't be seen organizing anything illegal. Too many questions if we weren't where we were meant to be, too much difficulty getting unmarked trucks up to where we stored the other stones. We met up, and agreed to play it cool for a few weeks. Wait for the investigation to die down. It wasn't as though we were in a rush, after all. We thought we had all the time in the world."

"And then Sam Acker was killed," I say, rubbing my chin.

"Yes. That was about when I realized what had happened. Somehow, the five of us had disturbed the Crocodile, and now it was coming after us."

"But Jim Thatch didn't disturb the Crocodile."

"We don't know that," Driscoll says. "He might have stumbled across the field, and not known what it was, or he could have found a stone that we missed and taken it with him. He wasn't that far away from our site, after all. And the next death – Sam, I mean. He died close to our western camp, in a straight line from the other two sites."

"And that was when you started hearing the ticking," I say.

"And when the Crocodile started destroying things, yes. I think it knows. It wants something from me. Maybe to lead it back to the stones. When it gets them, or gets tired of waiting, it's going to tear me apart."

"I have a simpler theory," I say after a moment. "I think one of your companions did the math, and decided that five shares was a lot more money than six. And if five shares, why not four? If you panic and run away, the others can split that money up nice and easy."

"You think one of them killed Sam?" Driscoll stares at me.

"Maybe, maybe not. He was in the woods, so it might have been the Crocodile that ate him. I definitely agree that it's out there. But think about it; it was out *there*. Still near the place where Thatch and Acker died, and near the original graveyard. I still don't think it had a way to reach your bushes without destroying your fence, and having seen it in action, I don't think it's subtle enough to wait for you to lead it somewhere. If it wanted to eat you, it would have tried by now. No, Mr. Driscoll, I very much think one of your co-conspirators is trying to scare you off, and I intend to figure out which one."

"And the crime itself?"

I shrug. "I'm not the police. If you aren't hurting anyone, I don't much care. I would recommend that you and your friends 'discover' this find some time soon, though, wherever you ended up hiding it. There's been too much attention drawn to it already. I would say you can make it look like Sam was planning to report the find when he died, take the money you've already stolen, and count yourselves lucky if no one looks more deeply into it. If there's no find, there's no one willing to kill over it."

Driscoll has the good grace not to argue with me, although from his expression I'm sure that I've hit a nerve. "Are you sure it's one of the others? I just can't believe it."

"Well, not necessarily. It could be someone else here, who's learned about your find and wants to steal it from you. For the moment, I'm sticking with the smaller list of suspects."

"Then I'm safe," Driscoll says, slowly smiling. "The Crocodile isn't after me!"

"First off, it might be. It just hasn't found its way into town. I would avoid any deep woods for the time being." As Driscoll's face falls, I decide to pile on the bad news while I can. "And secondly, safe isn't the word I would use."

"But if it's a hoax…"

"Someone killed Sam Acker. It could be that it was the Crocodile that did it, and that's what gave your tormentor the idea. Or it could be that someone killed Sam Acker, and used the recent death of Thatch to cover it up. Like you said, this is the find of a lifetime. People have killed for much less. Until I've figured this out, you need to be careful. I don't like losing clients."

"So what happens now?"

"Now," I say with a sigh, "comes the difficult part. I need to speak with your friends."

"They're not going to like that," Driscoll mutters.

As it turns out, he's more than right. After a short conversation, we agree to stick with the Jim Thatch story for the time being. It gives me a chance to interview people without having to drag a variety of major felonies into the mix, and might keep our fake crocodile from panicking. Of course, I don't have any legal authority to do these interviews, so my first stop has to be Ralph Ellis. I tailor my argument somewhat for him.

"You think someone's trying to steal our find?" Ralph asks, brow furrowed.

"It seems likely," I say.

"And I suppose you want a cut to solve the problem," he sneers. "I know your type, buddy, and you aren't getting a plugged nickel from me."

"Mr. Ellis," I say, "I resent that. I'm on a job right now, trying to solve a murder. And frankly, I get more than enough trouble from the police without being wrapped up in whatever 'fool-proof' scheme you've got cooked up."

"Sure, buddy, I bet you do." Ralph glares at me. "Well, congratulations. There's a big damned crocodile in the woods eating people. Murder solved. Get off our property."

"A crocodile with an uncanny interest in starstone. I wonder if I could find your stash just by following it around for a few days."

"Please try. Really, just get as close to it as you like." Ralph narrows his eyes at me. "I made some calls while you were cornering Driscoll. What are you really after, anyway? You're no crocodile hunter. You're a detective. A pirate, a few people said."

"Like I said, Mr. Ellis, I'm looking to solve a murder, and I suspect that your scheme is at its root. Who else did you bring in on this? I understand you bribed some dock workers, and I assume you spoke with certain other corporations. Were any of their agents on the island? The temptation to steal your cache could drive someone to take action."

"Don't be an idiot. There's no agents, there's no murderers, there's no one trying to put pressure on us except you." He shakes his head. "You want to talk to people, feel free. It'll probably make the loggers feel better to know there's some kind of guy looking into this who's more on their level. But you aren't going to find anything, because there's nothing to find. Giant crocodile. End of story."

"Not quite the end of the story," I say. "What was Sam Acker doing out in the woods alone?"

"Eh?"

"Surveyors always work in pairs," I point out.

"Maybe he was hoping for another find. One he wouldn't have to share."

"After a wild beast killed someone right next door?"

"Maybe I don't give a damn what he was doing out there!" Ralph shouts. "It was a damned shame that he got killed, but you're right, he shouldn't have been in the woods alone. He acted stupid, he got killed. Law of the jungle."

"Your concern is touching," I said dryly.

"Get out of my office. Go bother someone else."

I decide to take him up on his offer, before he actually gets angry enough to have security escort me off-site. After all, there are still people that I need to talk to, as soon as I can pin them down. First, I check in with Betty Wescoff.

I find her just outside the office of upper management, sitting in a chair and staring blankly at a wall. "Oh, hello, um…" She hesitates.

"Basil," I say smoothly. "Are you off duty? You look like you could use a drink."

"Well… alright, but only because we almost died earlier." Betty stands up, and we make our way downstairs to the cafeteria. Fortunately, there's plenty of beer on sale, and even a few bottles of cheap wine. I grab one, and a couple of glasses, and we sit down.

"The actual Crocodile. I never thought that I would see it," Betty says, taking taking a long drink.

"I was rather hoping to never see it again," I say. "You only get lucky so many times."

"You've seen the Crocodile before?" Betty pauses, looking at me, and I shrug.

"Once or twice. It ate one of my bosses, once."

"Wow. I'm sorry."

"I'm not. He was a monster. Honestly, they deserved each other. But I'd glad it didn't eat anyone this time around."

"Other than the logger, and the surveyor," Betty points out.

"Well, yes, I meant in this encounter." I sigh. "I suppose you're right, though. Damned shame."

"Management isn't inclined to shut down the camp. They've cordoned off a few zones near the attack sites, but they seem to think that the Crocodile won't roam far."

"I doubt that very much," I say thoughtfully. "I think it's going to keep roaming until it finds what it's looking for. Might take it some time, but it's awake now, and it doesn't seem too interested in going back to sleep."

"And you think it's after whoever stole that starstone."

I blink, staring at her. "I don't recall saying that."

"But it's obvious, if you look at the clues. Fragments of starstone, a clear impact site, tire tracks, angry Crocodile. Someone found some stones, and didn't report them. And now the Crocodile's after them, trying to get them back." Betty stares down at her wine. "The stories say that once it has a taste of something it never stops coming after them, and it definitely got a taste of those stones."

"Well, it may have already eaten them. Two dead people, after all, and then it went back home." I the wine in my glass around, staring down into it, and fighting the urge to down the whole thing and chase it with the bottle. I need my wits about me. "Both of them were in the area." I look up at her. "Why were you down there, Ms. Wescoff?"

"The reports didn't line up. There was no reason for the lumber to be as thin as they reported, unless the ground wasn't right, and if the ground wasn't right there should have been mineral deposits. I assumed the surveyors had just made a mistake. That they weren't looking closely, saw some poor trees, and decided to call it in, and that if I went down I could take some core samples and double-check them. But then I arrived and found the tire tracks, and then the starstone, and then…" She shudders. "And then the Crocodile."

"And then you grabbed a rifle and tried to save my life," I chuckle.

Betty puts her head in her hands. "Don't remind me. What was I thinking?"

"You weren't, I expect. You were reacting." I pat her on the shoulder, standing up. "There are worse reactions to have. Thank you."

She looks up at me. "No, thank you, Mr. Stark. Somehow, I don't think that rifle would have done us much good. You saved all our lives."

"Just in the right place at the right time. And please, call me Basil. Finish your drink, take some rest. Trust me from experience, you're going to need it."

She laughs. "You're a very odd man, Basil. Have a good night."

I leave my wineglass behind, untouched, and move on. Betty is sharp, and there's an even chance that she's going to end up getting someone arrested if Driscoll and his crew don't take my advice and abandon their plan, but that's not my problem, and I don't have her pegged as a killer.

The next one on my list is Jake Collins, and I find him at his desk, working on another survey site. He's about as pleased to see me as Ralph was. "What the hell do you want?"

"Just to speak with you. Do you have a minute?"

Jake gestures to his desk, which is covered in papers. "Do I look like I have a minute? I've got a half-dozen of Sam's old sites to check up on, and now we have to deal with cordoning off every site within half a mile of that Crocodile attack this evening. Nice job with that, by the way."

I can't tell if he's being sarcastic or not, so I choose to believe the best. "Well, no one died this time," I agree.

"Damned Crocodile. Seems like it's everywhere all of a sudden," Collins mutters.

"And it may stay there," I warn him, sitting down next to his desk and lowering my voice. "It was very interested in the starstone I found."

Collins goes very still. "You found a starstone?" he says carefully.

"Yes, damndest thing. I believe Ms. Wescoff included it in her report to management," I say. "It seems like that's what the Crocodile was looking for. I don't suppose you noticed anything like that when you were out there?"

"Me?" Collins laughs nervously. "I don't know what you're talking about."

"Maybe we should continue this conversation in private," I suggest, "before someone wonders why you're suddenly sweating."

"Fine," Collins snarls, standing up. A few people look over in surprise, and he lowers his voice. "Fine," he repeats. "Follow me."

Collins leads me to a supply room, and carefully locks the door. "So what's your big secret?"

"I know about your cache," I say. "And I know that Sam Acker was in on it."

Collins crumples. "Andrew! That goddamn idiot. How much did he tell you?"

"Just about everything, eventually. "Look, Mr. Collins, I'm trying to help, here, but I need to know more about the find."

"Because you think that's what the Crocodile wants?" Collins snorts. "Andrew's been telling us all his little ghost stories. They're not real. He's just afraid because Sam died."

"And you aren't?"

"I'm not planning to go out into the woods alone, let alone with starstone in my pockets."

That catches my attention. "Sam had starstone with him? In the woods?"

"He must have," Collins says with a shrug. "We were down a few pieces. Dumb bastard."

"What would he have been doing with it?"

"Damned if I know. And frankly, I don't care. Never much liked him anyway."

"Maybe you should be more concerned. There must have been a reason for him to do that, and it could be a clue to why he died."

"Maybe you should leave me the hell alone," Collins snaps. "Sam died because he was an idiot, and because he got too close to a site where someone had already been killed. Look, Andrew brought you in to look into things, because he's a panicky little baby, but I'm not. Whatever hallucinations the man's been having are none of my concern, because that Crocodile isn't going to get anywhere near us, because we are not going anywhere near the western woods. Now if you'll kindly piss the hell off, I have real work to do."

"Got it," I say. "Until next time, then."

Since Collins is determined to ignore my advice, I move on to my last target. I don't have to go far; she finds me as I'm leaving the supply room.

"Mr. Stark," Kathryn Zhang says, bearing down on me. "Still skulking around the place, I see."

"Ms. Zhang," I reply, with a nod. "Just the woman I was looking for. Do you mind if we talk, privately?"

"Why not?" she asks. "You were rude enough in public, I can't imagine it will get any worse." She leads me right back into the room Collins and I left, closing the door behind her, and then leans against it.

"Cozy little place," I say. "Do you have all your secret meetings here?"

"No one uses it, much. I heard you had a run-in with a monster."

"One or two. Seems Driscoll was right to be concerned."

Kathryn snorts. "I suppose he's babbled everything to you by now."

"Between him and Ralph Ellis, I have a pretty good idea about what's been happening. Do you?"

"I don't know what you mean, Basil." Kathryn examines her nails, the picture of boredom.

"Two people are already dead because of this find of yours. And this afternoon, if Amos and I hadn't arrived when we did, it would have been four. Doesn't that worry you, even a little?"

"I don't agree with your premise. What happened to Sam, and to that logger, was a tragedy. I don't know what he was thinking, going out into the woods alone like that, but it doesn't change the fact that he's dead, and I miss him. But the Crocodile arriving when it did was a coincidence. It's not out looking for us."

"It seemed pretty interested in the starstone I threw at it."

"I heard that story, too," Kathryn says dryly. "You threw a rock at its head. It attacked the rock. Seems like pretty normal beast behaviour to me; no need to drag anything else into it."

"So you're not planning to abandon the cache, then?"

"Well, for the time being, we're going to have to," Kathryn admits. "Far too much attention. But no, once the Crocodile moves on, I plan to keep things going, and the others feel the same. Except for Driscoll, who's had an attack of the nerves."

"Nerves didn't trample his rose bed," I say.

"He might have, just to have evidence to present to you," she counters. "You don't seriously think that the Crocodile wandered down into the suburbs, leaned against Andrew's house, and then got bored and wandered off, do you? I've been to Andrew's house, and it would not stop an angry Crocodile."

"You're probably right," I say. "It seems pretty unlikely that the Crocodile did that."

"Well, then…" Kathryn trails off. "You think one of us did it?"

I shrug. "Someone did, and I can't imagine Driscoll hiring me to investigate himself."

'Hmph," Kathryn shakes her head. "I think you're barking up the wrong tree, Basil. A neighbor's dog probably just tore up Driscoll's garden, and he panicked. I don't think he's cut out for all this cloak and dagger business. But hey, it's not my money. If you want to join Driscoll in his fantasies, be my guest. Waste your time and his money as long as you like; hell, maybe you'll actually end up making the poor guy feel better. Just keep it out of my business." Straightening, she opens the door. "And don't let Ralph catch you riling up the workers. We've got enough trouble as it is."

"Your concern is touching," I say dryly as the door slams behind her.

There's nothing else to do here for the moment, so I let Driscoll know that I'll be back tomorrow, after I carry on some investigations elsewhere, and catch a bus heading back into town. I stop by the office before it closes to check for messages and equip myself for the evening, and fill Holly in on the details while I'm there.

"Geez, Uncle Basil," she says, shaking her head. "That's a hell of a day you just had."

"I've had worse."

"I've seen some of them, but that doesn't make this one good." Holly taps her pencil against her desk. "So the Crocodile's really after Driscoll?"

"The Crocodile is really after someone, but I don't think it's the main threat in this little farce. I think our villain, whomever he or she is, decided to use that to their advantage and try and scare Driscoll off. He's probably not in any real danger, aside from the threat of not getting a good night's sleep."

"Well, that's good news, at least." Holly nods, leaning forwards. "Who do you think did it?"

"Hard to say. It could be any of his co-conspirators. But I have an idea I want to track down, tonight. There might be more than one way to go about this."

"Let me see if I can guess it. You aren't going to get them to admit it, so… you're going to stalk Driscoll?"

"Good idea, but no. Too soon. None of them would be dumb enough to try to scare him the day he hires a private investigator. They're all convinced he's making things up – or at least, two of them are, and the third wants me to be convinced. They'll lay low for a few days." I shake my head. "My thought is that if one of Driscoll's friends is getting greedy, they might have gotten greedy in more ways than one. Snagged a few pieces of iron for themselves, and sold it on the sly." I cross over to the office's small safe, and pull out a hundred dollars in small bills, and a pistol.

"That seems kind of like a dumb idea." Holly glances at the pistol, raising an eyebrow, but doesn't comment on it directly.

"You would think that," I agree, tucking it into my coat. "But first off, I have my doubts about the brains of anyone involved in this caper, and secondly, Collins actually suggested it. He said that there was some starstone missing, which he assumed that Sam Acker took with him to the woods. That seems like bad planning even by the standards of this group, so…"

"So you think someone else has been skimming off the top," Holly finishes, nodding. "I can see it happening."

"And if I can track down who the thief is, I expect to have a strong lead on who tricked Sam Acker into the woods."

"Wait," Holly says slowly. "Someone tricked him?"

"He had no reason to be out there alone. That's something that everyone has agreed on, that he should have had someone else with him. Hawthorne always sends people out in pairs."

"Wouldn't there have been a record of him going out with someone else?"

"Not if they removed it. Anyway, it's still all just a hunch. Hopefully, when I manage to track down the thief, I'll be able to upgrade to a theory."

"And what should I be doing, while you're out investigating the seedy underbelly of the city?"

"Go home and get some sleep. I assume you've been here all day."

"Well, yeah, but I could come along and help…"

"And then you would need to find a new job, because your mother would literally murder me," I point out.

Holly looks like she's considering an attempt at pouting, but instead she just sighs and nods. "Fine," she says, "but you'd better tell me the whole story tomorrow."

I grin and grab my hat. "All of the salacious details," I promise.

The Treehouse is the foremost nightclub of medium-ill intent in the city of Everland. Decades ago, it was a literal tree house – the hidden fortress of the Lost Boys, its entrances perfectly sculpted to their bodies and its interior a massive playground for their games. When the colonists arrived, and the Pan lost his war against them and fled, the last of the Lost Boys were returned to society. They live somewhere between unfortunate addicts and beloved celebrities – the Orphans, as they came to be known, never quite adapted to the new world, although those that chose to stay have managed to get by. They've all found places near the edges of society, and I don't have much interaction with any of them – with one exception. Brandon Fisher, who cheerfully calls himself the Fisher King, laid claim to the Treehouse on behalf of his fellow Orphans, and then gradually bought them out. These days it's a nightclub, casino, meeting place for shady business deals, and neutral ground in the city's occasional gang fights. Everland's foremost gang lord has made it clear that violence in the Treehouse would end badly for all involved, so the minor gangs and conspiracies that mostly obey him have followed suit.

I'm a known factor at the Treehouse, and have a free pass to come and go as I please after a few favours I did for Brandon in the bad old days, so his bouncers only delay me for a minute or so while they confiscate my pistol and confirm that it's my only weapon. That done, they gesture to one of the wooden tunnels that serve as elevators into the club, and I tip my hat to them as I walk by.

The interior is, as always, dark and what passes for romantic these days. There's no smoking inside, due to the whole building being made of living wood, but that never seems to change the ambiance. Low electric lights are carefully set up to leak out from hidden alcoves. There are no windows inside, only thin slits for the wind to whistle softly through. The effect is frankly a bit haunting, meant to evoke the awe and fear everyone has for the old days, with fairy-lights and coiling dry smoke along the ground. Slow jazz music plays from speakers tucked into folds in the tree, and the tables are crowded with evening club-goers sharing drinks and stories.

Brandon catches me only a few feet from the door. "Basil, buddy!" he cries, striding over. He has a glass of wine in one hand and an unlit cigar in the other, which he waves in my direction. "When they said you were here I hardly believed it. It's been months!"

"Brandon," I say politely. "How have you been?"

"Oh, business is booming, my friend. Come on over to the bar, let's have a drink and see if I can give you a hand with your case."

"You know I'm on a case?"

"Basil," Brandon says with a grin, "when you deign to visit me, you're always on a case. Usually an exciting one.

So come on, spill. Which gang should I stop investing in before you leave them groaning on the pavement?"

I can't help but laugh at that one. "You may know the answer to that one before I do, this time." We head over to the bar, and Brandon orders me a glass of white wine. It seems impolite to refrain, but I leave it sitting on the bar for the moment. "This may sound like an odd question, Brandon, but I'm here about starstone."

"Starstone?" Brandon frowns. "You're right, that sounds weird as hell. Why not ask your buddies up the Hill?"

I wince. "I think it might be better to keep Second Star out of this one," I say. "Anyway, it would be a stretch to call them 'buddies'. I have one or two friends there, but they aren't exactly running the business, and you and I both know that the Powers That Be aren't supporters."

"Yeah, I've never gotten that," Brandon says, shaking his head. "The Darlings are always giving me and the club a pass, and ragging on you like it's going out of style. We're all Neverlanders together."

"You can say that, you lived after my pirate days," I point out. "I was just the strange man living with the Indians, to you, keeping my head down and avoiding the Pan."

"Still, man, it's not like you chose to come here any more than any of us," Brandon says, shaking his head. "Whatever, if I knew what went on in a lawman's head I'd be rich."

I raise my eyebrows, and take a small sip of the wine.

"Alright, richer," Brandon says. "What do you need to know about starstone?"

"Who's been selling it on the black market, mainly."

"Now, hold on a minute, Basil," Brandon says, putting down his cigar. "The Treehouse is neutral turf, and one of the ways I keep it that way is not talking about deals that go on around here. If I tell you that, the next thing you know someone wants to have words with me about turning over their suppliers, and then they find me floating in the harbour."

"They wouldn't do that. Everyone loves you."

"Like hell they do. I'm on a tightrope here, and you come along to push me off. Starstone's a controlled substance. The people that buy it don't want Second Star messing around their turf, and I can't see this info helping you without coming to light."

"I don't care about buyers, Brandon. It's sellers that interest me. Think of it as if you were setting me up to make a buy. Heck, I might even pick up a piece or two. They could come in handy in the near future, I think."

"What the hell do you want starstone for?"

"Crocodile distraction."

Brandon gives me a funny look. "Right," he says slowly. "Okay, look. I don't usually set up deals directly, but as it happens I do have a few pieces of starstone on hand. Personally, see? Got it from a client with a bit of a gambling problem, in lieu of cash. Not a bad bargain, if I do say so myself. Thing is, I just had somebody in here half hour ago asking the same questions as you. Wanted to get a hold of some starstone, curious about the seller. These things make me nervous, you see?"

"And what did you say to this mystery person?"

"I told her the same thing I'm going to tell you. You want to buy some rocks, I can do business. But my clients' secrets are their own."

"And?"

"And she bought the goods. I only had three left, and she took them all away with her."

"Come on, Brandon, throw me a line, here," I say. "Let me talk to the client. Maybe I can persuade him to give me his source."

"Damn it, Basil," Brandon rubs his forehead.

"Brandon, this is serious. Two people are dead, and the Crocodile is on the loose. The real one. The Regulators are going to start looking into things, and I expect them to come down on everyone involved like a ton of bricks. If I'm going to get my own client loose from it, I need to have the whole case wrapped up and tied with a bow before then."

"The Regulators." Brandon pales. "Damn it, Basil! Why didn't you lead with that?"

"I didn't want to worry you."

"Too goddamn late! Alright, fine. You go and talk to the supplier, and I'll make sure there's no trace of him ever coming here, but you've got to do something for me."

"I'm listening."

"Find that lady who came in earlier, and make sure she's not planning to rat me out. Get her out of the line of fire, or something. The last thing I need is Regulators breathing down my throat because she causes a fuss, or the cops doing it because something happens to her. My bribes only go so far."

I chuckle. "You have my word. Just give me the names."

"The dame was trying to be cagey, but she was, frankly, no good at it. My guys palmed her wallet while she was talking to me, got her ID. Betty Wescoff. She's still hanging around the club, last I checked."

"Well, she moves fast. But it could be worse. I'll have a word. And the gambler?"

"Sam Acker. Nice fellow, but terrible at the dice."

I blink. "Sorry. Sam Acker? Are you sure?"

"Absolutely. He's a regular." Brandon catches my expression. "There a problem?"

I drain the wine sitting next to me. "There certainly is. He was eaten by a crocodile."

"Damn," Brandon says slowly. "I'll miss him. Good source of cash."

"And," I growled, "it leaves me right back where I started. No one could have killed him to cover up their thefts if he was the one stealing." I stand. "Thank you for the help, Brandon."

"Just talk to the lady, alright? And take care of yourself. That monster's a bad one, and you're a good guy to know, Basil."

"I'll do my best," I say, as I walk away.

It only takes a few minutes to find Ms. Wescoff. She's hovering by the blackjack tables, talking to another patron, a sweaty-faced man who's gesturing wildly, repeatedly coming close to spilling his drink. She's nodding intently, leaning in to listen closely, while he talks at some length. I glance around, deciding to give her a minute, and settle in a few feet away to listen in. Neither she nor he notice me, and I wave the waitress off as she approaches.

The man is talking about someone he's played games with in the past, waxing poetic about some grand game that took place. "You should have seen it," he slurs. "Cool as a cucumber. Just put his chips down, didn't even look at the cards. Then he bought a round for everyone with the winnings. Damndest thing."

"And the night of the fight?"

"Oh, yeah, he came in all flustered. The bouncers were hovering right next to him, like he was about to get tossed, but he just walked over to Eddie," the man gestured towards one corner, "and walked into the back with him."

"And came back with more chips," Betty says seriously. Out of the corner of my eye, I noticed another guy lounging a little too casually. He's taken at least five sips from his martini, but it hasn't dropped a hair. And he doesn't look much like a patron – he's built like a truck, and he keeps glancing over in Betty's direction and then back towards a table near the edge of the room, where two more guys are glancing back.

"And won a couple more rounds, yeah," the guy says. "Dunno how he got Eddie to give him all that money, but it sure worked out."

"That's a pretty good story," Betty agrees. "Have another drink, I'll be right back."

"Lovely to hear it, honey. You're good luck." The man turns back to the table as she walks away. The guy with the martini makes a gesture, and another guy from the table gets up to follow her.

I decide it's time to get involved. "Ms. Wescoff," I say, falling into step beside her. The tough that's walking forward pauses, then matches steps with us, staying a few feet back. "Fancy meeting you here."

"Well, hello, Basil. Now I know I'm on the right track."

"The right track to a serious beating, maybe. There are some goons behind me looking for a word, and I don't think they're inclined to follow the rules. Have you seriously been asking about Eddie Lake?"

"More than asking. I've thought this through, Basil. I've got a trail, and I found out some good intel. I talked to someone who offered to put me in touch with Eddie to buy some starstone, and you'll never guess who else spoke to him."

"Sam Acker."

Betty's face falls. "How did you figure that out?"

"Bypassed the middle man. It has its advantages." I walk Betty slowly towards the exit. "For one thing, my way doesn't result in someone mentioning to Eddie Lake that you were asking about him."

"Is he trouble?"

"Betty, he is specifically a dealer in the sort of goods that Second Star prefers to keep under wraps. He's been arrested seventeen times and never convicted. No witnesses." I shake my head. "He keeps enough goons around to make your night very unpleasant in the very near future, and I will be delighted to learn about your cunning plan to avoid that."

"Well… this is neutral ground, isn't it? No violence in the Treehouse?" Betty glances over her shoulder. There are definitely now three goons walking gradually towards us, and the bouncers are starting to take note. "I did some asking around."

"No violence in the Treehouse, but that doesn't mean that there's no violence near it. Especially if you don't have anyone to back you up. Before I showed up, I expect Eddie was hoping you didn't know that rule. He'd have his goons try to intimidate you into leaving with them, and then get you somewhere quiet. If you didn't go with it, he'd have them follow you. Same result. How are you at losing tails?"

"Well, I came in a car."

"That bad, huh." I sigh. "Did you park it outside?"

"Well… yes…"

"Did the bouncers outside see you park it?"

"Maybe."

"Chances are it's already got a flat tire." I shake my head. "Alright, we try this another way. Play along." I stop dead, and turn around, taking several steps towards our pursuers. "Gentlemen."

"Stark," one of the three goons says. He glowers at me. "Walk away."

"Or?" There isn't an immediate reaction, and I smile, taking another step towards them. "My reputation precedes me, I see."

"You think you can take us?"

"I think I can raise a ruckus." I reach over, patting the thug on the shoulder. "You know the fuzz always has someone watching the tunnels. They marked me the moment I came in, and they'll be watching for me coming out. There's no way out of here without being spotted, and you're not dealing with riff-raff right now. My partner here is proper society. If she goes missing, there's a lot of heat, and Eddie doesn't want that. And if you make noise, the police will descend on you. I can handle being arrested. It happens to me all the time. Eddie's on thinner ice. I don't think he'd be too pleased if you create a scene and get him thrown out of the Treehouse once and for all."

The thug cracks his knuckles, and a beefy hand closes on my shoulder as one of his friends steps forward. "Maybe we should go and let Eddie decide that."

"Maybe you should step off," I suggest, as the bouncers by the door straighten up and start watching us intently. "Unless you want a fight with the whole staff."

There is a tense pause, and then the thug holding me lets go. I turn, patting him on the cheek, and then step back before he can explode. "Good boy. Come on, Betty, we're leaving."

"Sure thing, Basil," Betty says coolly.

I straighten my back, spin on one foot, and stride for the doorway. Betty follows right behind me, leaving three very uncertain thugs glaring after us. Under her breath, she says, "Okay, what now?"

"That depends. Are you wearing heels?"

"Flats. I guessed my night might include running."

"Good guess. First, we take this tunnel outside. Then we break into a sprint, flag down a cab, and get the hell out of here before Tweedle, Dee, and Dumb back there get themselves together and come after us."

"You don't think they bought your story?"

"Oh, they bought it." I gesture quietly. "They're sending someone back to talk to Eddie, and I already know what he's going to say. He's been looking for a chance to try and mess me up without looking like a sore loser."

"So you're saying I'm in more trouble now than before you swept in," Betty says.

"Well… let's say you're in different trouble. If I'd realized which Eddie you were talking about earlier, I wouldn't have barged in quite so quickly." We reach the tunnels, and I spare her a smile. "Ready to run?"

"You seem to do that a lot," Betty says sourly.

I nod, claiming my coat and stepping into the tunnel. The wood closes around me, drawing me up to street level, and I check my pockets for my things. A moment later, Betty pops out, pulling her own coat around her. She nods, I nod back, and we take off like the dogs of hell are in pursuit. I spot a cab coming around the corner, and wave it down, and the two of us pile into the back just as a trio of identically-dressed thugs emerge from the entrance of the club. "To the corner of Jane and Hale!" I shout to the driver, "and step on it!"

Betty collapses against the side of the car, giggling as we speed away. The thugs are all waving wildly and shouting, breaking into a run, and she takes a moment to wave back as we leave them in the dust. As they double back for their own car, she shakes her head. "Are they going to try to chase us?" she asks.

"Oh, they're going to try," I say with a grin, reaching into my pocket and pulling out a set of car keys. "Right about now, Goon #2 is probably realizing that his pockets are a little light."

"What… when did you…" Betty's eyes narrow. "Did you seriously pick his pockets in the middle of that confrontation?"

"Well, I sure as hell wasn't going to win if we got into a punching match. Did you see the size of those goons? They'd have wiped the floor with me." I toss the keys out the window. "Anyway, they'll have to go and tell Eddie what happened, or else hotwire their own car. Either way, we're in the clear."

"Wow, you sure know how to dial up a girl's evening."

I turn to grin at her. "Why, Ms. Wescoff, I think it's possible that you may secretly be a hellion."

"Why, Mr. Stark, whatever do you mean? I'm just an innocent young engineer. You, on the other hand, seem to have a real need to swoop in and save the day."

"I think of it as more of a curse. But maybe I can make up for it. Have you ever had pie at Jessie's?"

"It doesn't sound familiar."

"Then you're in for a treat."

The cab drops us off outside Jessie's Fine Dining and Family-Friendly Restaurant, a hangout particularly popular with off-duty police officers and local night owls. A few of them give me the stink-eye as I stroll in, a few others nod to me in a more or less friendly way, and we find our way to an empty booth. I order a couple of slices of pie from the waiter, and after a moment, I add a pair of root beers to the list.

"So, Ms. Wescoff," I say seriously, "I think we need to talk."

"It's still Betty," she reminds me. "And I think you're right. Why don't you start with why you're helping to cover up a crime?"

"Priorities. First off, my goal is prevent more killings, not to help the police arrest a few workers. Secondly, and I hope you don't take this the wrong way, but I don't really care for Hawthorne Logging. They chew through the island without any real idea of what they're upsetting, they tear apart sacred lands with no concern for the cost, and they rely on connections to the government to pay their workers poorly and let them by with no oversight. If something like this were happening at Second Star, the Regulators would have solved the problem by now, but Hawthorne doesn't care how many people die if they can keep the lumber coming."

Betty sits back in her seat. "Well. You're not shy about your opinions, at least."

"It's not everyone there. Plenty of people who work at Hawthorne are pleasant – I play cards with some of them every weekend. But your upper management is rotten to the core." I shake my head. "Can I hazard a guess about something? You spoke with them, and they told you they would close off a few areas, but you should leave everything else to the police, and no sense worrying them about a couple of starstone pieces. They may even have suggested that you shouldn't have been out at the site alone."

"Well… yes," Betty admits. "To all of it. How did you know?"

"Because if you thought the police were following up, you wouldn't have bothered to look up the Treehouse," I say dryly. "And also because I'm almost certain that Ralph Ellis's secret connections are, in fact, Hawthorne's upper management."

Betty blinks. "What?"

"This whole scheme is absolutely untenable otherwise. A surveyor makes a find and talks to his boss, who just happens to know someone who can sell starstone on the black market, in vast quantities?" I snort. "Ellis doesn't want the others to know, because the fact that they think they're hiding from their own company means he can undervalue the goods, pay upper management a strong cut, and still skim off the top. But come on – a five percent finder's fee? On absolutely untraceable, highly valuable discoveries? That's what you do when you *want* your employees to cheat you. Or when you want to cheat your shareholders, using your employees as patsies." I shrug. "I wouldn't trust you either, except that you obviously ignored warnings and started stirring things up. I can't see a reason for you to do that if you were involved, so I figure you're probably clean."

Betty is staring at me, pie forgotten. "They couldn't have that kind of infrastructure set up!" she protests. "How would they know this find was coming?"

"Why do you think this is a new trick?" I counter. "Do some digging, and I suspect you'll find a surprisingly high turnover rate among the surveyors. Hawthorne and Second Star have never gotten along, and I expect this was just one more branch of that little war. As long as the supervisors were corrupt, they could steer the surveyors to commit crimes, feed a steady stream of starstone to Second Star's corporate enemies, and feather their own nests. Totally unprovable, of course."

"Unless we get Ralph Ellis to talk," Betty interjects.

"His word against his bosses. I guarantee they aren't letting him keep a paper trail." I shake my head. "No, my goal here is to figure out who killed Acker, hand them over to the police, save my client, and then let the Commissioner try to untangle the unsolvable Case of The Stolen Starstone." I chuckle. "He won't thank me for it."

"God," Betty says. "That's… really cynical."

"Welcome to the world of corporate fraud. If it weren't for the deaths, the whole thing would be laughable."

"So who killed Thatch and Acker?"

"Well, I think the Crocodile killed Thatch. He was just in the wrong place at the wrong time. It's possible that he was one of the people Ellis hired to move some starstone, or maybe he just found a couple of pieces. Either way, he got in its path and got eaten. But Acker…" I shake my head. "I have suspicions, but I don't have any proof yet. It was definitely one of his co-conspirators. Someone found out that he was skimming, got upset, and killed him. Possibly by mistake, possibly carefully, I'm not sure. I'm almost certain that it was either Collins or Zhang; the amounts wouldn't be enough to really upset Ellis, and Acker wouldn't have gone into the woods with his supervisor. Whichever one did it, they probably thought about the Crocodile sighting, and tried to make the crime scene look like a croc attack. And Hawthorne was so revved up to cover up that the Crocodile was back, and to get things calmed down so they could ship their starstone out and make a fortune, they didn't bother to do any investigating. All the proof that Acker was murdered got wiped out by people who thought they were covering up something else entirely." I pause to take a bite of pie. "Again, a comedy of errors."

"So what's the plan now?"

"For me, the plan is to keep up the pressure. As for you... the best thing for you to do would be to finish your pie, go home, get some sleep, and forget the investigation entirely. You will, at best, lose your job if you're even slightly responsible for Hawthorne getting a bloody nose, and there's an even chance that's where this is going. Not to mention the real possibility of getting killed by either a murderer, or a crocodile."

"Not a chance. Two people are dead, Basil. I can't just sit back and ignore that."

"You don't trust me to handle it alone?" I ask. Betty's glare is answer enough. "Alright, then. You're in."

"Really?"

"Yes, really. Don't sound so surprised. Honestly, I could use the help. The more people I can claim to be visiting at Hawthorne, the better."

"I thought I was going to have to put up more of a fight to get in, that's all."

"In my experience, when someone gets that particular set to their jaw, they're someone I would rather have within eyesight."

Betty laughs. "Smart man. In which case I repeat – what's the plan?"

I consider. "We'll want to meet up first thing tomorrow. I'll stop by on some trumped-up excuse, to meet with you." I rub my chin. "Maybe you called for me, to talk about the Crocodile thing?"

"After all," Betty says, "we didn't get much of a chance to talk when it happened. And we have not, of course, been visiting nightclubs. That would be just scandalous."

"Of course," I agree. "That's the sort of thing that hellions do, not innocent young engineers. So, we will officially be leaving to go up into the woods again. Unofficially, we will be checking the records to see what we can shake loose; mysterious sector closings, unusual purchases, that sort of thing. I can get into the filing rooms, but I'll need your help with the files. You'll have a better idea of what is or isn't strange than me."

"Sounds solid. Come by at 9:00, no sense in you scaring management by being around before then."

I pick up my hat, and stand. "For now, madam, do you mind if I walk you home? Not that I think that you need it, but…"

"But with crooks on the street looking for me, you feel safer that way?" Betty says. She takes my outstretched hand. "Mr. Stark, it would be my pleasure."

The next day, sadly, isn't nearly as pleasant as the previous was. The sun is hiding between thick, grey clouds, and a spatter of rain intermittently drips onto the city, not enough to wash it clean, but plenty to make everyone short-tempered and damp. I grab my greatcoat and a wide-brimmed hat, and venture out into the cold autumn, wishing for a brief interlude of summer as I flag down another taxi. One of these days, I should probably learn to drive; cars seem to be here to stay, and the city just keeps growing.

As the taxi drops me off outside Hawthorne Logging, I see that I'm not the only one here. Off to the side, near the half-empty parking lot, a large truck and three smaller offroad vehicles are set up, each one marked with the claw-and-wing sigil of the Regulators. A dozen men and women wearing heavy brown uniforms, each with the same sigil on its back, are in the process of checking over a wicked assortment of rifles, chemical throwers, and heavy shotguns. The smaller cars each have a vine-net launcher attached to their top – the edges of the vines twitch hungrily, straining to be released from their steel cages.

At a safe distance surrounding the Regulators, with a small band of police officers keeping the peace, are about forty shouting protesters, carrying homemade signs that read 'Neverland, Not Everland', or 'Leave the Forest to the Beast!' I spot the Pannite preacher from the other day near the front, screaming imprecations at the Regulators as they prepare to suit up. I can't quite make out what he's saying. Something about a divine punishment for the sins of logging, probably. The protesters are also largely blocking the front gate, and a half-dozen Hawthorne employees are in the middle of an argument with them. Spotting a couple that I recognize, I drift forward.

"Mr. Stark," Kathryn Zhang says, giving me a nod. "Back to bother us again, I see."

"I might not have the chance," I say, looking over the protesters. "What's all this?"

"Oh, the usual. The Regulators are suiting up to go hunt that crocodile you said you saw, and the usual collection of hippies, religious fanatics, and troublemakers are here to shout slogans." She points a short distance ahead, to where Jake Collins is in the middle of a heated argument with a protester wearing a necklace of feathers. "Jake's not taking it well."

Collins is, in fact, in the middle of an impressive rant. "I'd like to see you go after the Regulators when there's a tiger chewing on your leg!"

"That won't happen, because I don't believe in destroying their natural habitats!" the protester retorts. "There are no tigers on the shore lands, where we live in peace with the mermaids! Only here, where you tear apart their nests and kill their prey, do they come looking for human meat!"

"Wordy, isn't she?" Zhang says to me quietly.

"For once, we agree."

Collins, meanwhile, has clearly had enough. "Get out of my way. I have a job to get to!"

"Jobs despoiling the land, destroying our history for your corporate greed!" She steps towards him, physically blocking his path. He rears back and punches her in the gut.

As she falls down, eyes wide with shock, several protesters surge towards us, incensed by the violence, but the police are already here, and when it comes to Hawthorne or protesters, the North Precinct will always side with the group that gives their department huge 'donations' every year. They move quickly, grabbing anyone who tries to retaliate and shoving them to the ground. Beside me, Zhang is laughing quietly and shaking her head. Collins, trembling, pushes through the front gate before anyone else can stop him, and Zhang, nodding to me, follows.

I, unfortunately, am not wearing a Hawthorne uniform or badge, so I don't trust my ability to slip through the picket so easily. Instead, I back away from the confrontation and wait a few minutes for it to die down. It doesn't take long – most of the protesters are smart enough not to go after the cops, and after five or six people are arrested, things start to calm down. The Regulators, meanwhile, have finished suiting up, and drive into the woods, unnoticed by the people who arrived to yell at them as usual.

I wait for the police to drive off, and the protesters to start to disperse, and then present myself at the front gate once again, this time armed with my invitation from Betty Wescoff. The guard is suspicious for a moment, possibly trying to decide if I'm a protester with a new trick up my sleeve, but ultimately waves me through with the same warnings as the day before. I'm not actually sure that he remembers me. It's probably just as well.

Betty is waiting downstairs by the surveyor's office, a steaming mug in one hand. "Good morning, Basil," she says brightly. "Coffee?"

"Don't touch the stuff. The taste is much too bitter. I don't suppose that there's tea."

"We can probably find some," Betty says doubtfully.

"Never mind, I'll make do. Which way to the filing rooms?"

"Just down here, but there are two problems. Firstly, they are of course locked."

"That's less of a problem and more of a very short obstacle. What's the second?"

"Security patrols that area. How do we get past them?"

"Wiles?" I suggest. Betty gives me a withering look. "What? I'll have you know I have very good wiles."

"Of course you do," Betty sighs. "Do you have an actual plan?"

"Absolutely. We're looking for earlier reports about the area that's been roped-off, in order to determine if there were Crocodile sightings there in the past."

"And you think they'll buy it?"

"Why else would we have the key to the records room?"

"We don't have the key to the records room."

"We will after I pick someone's pocket. Come on."

"I am going to be arrested," Betty mutters as she follows me.

"You're not going to be arrested."

"End of my career."

"You're not going to be arrested."

"And they'll ask me, what were you doing, and I'll say, I don't know, the dashing older man tricked me with his smooth talk."

"Well, thank you for thinking that I'm dashing. Come on, we'll talk to the guards. Nip this whole project in the bud."

The process of getting a key is simplicity itself. First, I quietly drop my lighter on the floor. Then, a short distance further, I stop a guard and ask about the location of the records room, claiming to have official business there. I take the chance to lift his key ring from his belt, and walk away. Once Betty identifies the records room key, I slip it off the chain, return to ask the guard if he's seen my lighter, which as it happens he has. I return his key ring, one key short, as he returns my lighter, and we go our separate ways. By the time he notices the missing key – if he ever does – we'll be done with it, and I can leave it somewhere inconspicuous.

The records room itself is a bit intimidating; boxes and boxes of files, stacked on metal filing shelves, filling a long, dark room with a handful of tables for sorting through materials. A small doorway leads to the copying room, mostly taken up by a large Photostat machine, and a few high windows let in a little bit of grey light. I look around, nodding, and start looking for boxes.

"So, what exactly are we looking for?" Betty asks.

I pass her a scrap of paper. "Earlier Crocodile sightings. The unconfirmed ones, mostly, although I've gone back to a few of the confirmed ones, too. I want to see if they line up with other patterns of sites being declared non-viable without further research. Especially if those sites were opened up a few years later. Here are the years, and the rough locations the Crocodile was spotted. See if you can find anything."

"You really know how to treat a girl," Betty says, going for the first box.

"So you've mentioned."

We spend the next two hours pulling down boxes and sorting through them. At first, we aren't having much luck, but after about half an hour Betty spots a listing from 1949, opening up a site for logging. An earlier report listed it as no good, but a new survey suggests that the woods may have grown back sufficiently for logging. We track down the earlier report, from '44, and find a number of similarities between it and our current situation. Of particular note is the name of the surveyor who reported the site as useless – Ralph Ellis. A bit more digging reveals that his partner on the survey retired later that year, and moved to California.

Once we have a lead, we track it forward, and find a few more sites. We focus on sites surveyed by Ralph and his then-partner, and by the two who counter-signed. In five cases, which is nearly every time that the four of them survey as a set, we find irregularities. Four of the five are later opened for business. And while they don't all correspond to Crocodile sightings, four out of the six do, and five involve a logging accident within a few weeks that leads to one or two dead loggers.

"Jesus," Betty says, staring down at the reports. "The Crocodile really is following the graveyard discoveries."

"It certainly has an interest."

"Do you think he's noticed?" she asks. "Ralph, I mean?"

I frown. "I can't imagine that he hasn't. He may have convinced himself that it's a coincidence, but nearly every time he conceals a find, someone dies. It's happened too often to overlook."

"What happens too often to overlook?"

I curse under my breath, and look up. "Ms. Zhang," I say politely. "What brings you down here?"

"I heard a guard complaining that management had people looking in the filing room," she says evenly. "Imagine my surprise to find out it was you, given that you do not work here."

"I'm just lending a hand to a friend," I say, gesturing to Betty.

"Really," Kathryn says.

"Absolutely," Betty agrees. She smiles broadly. "I was just trying to see if there'd been any Crocodile sightings near the site in the last few years. You know, if we could figure out what its range was, we might be able to get a few sectors open again." She sighs. "I just feel so responsible for all those loggers, since I found the Crocodile in the first place."

"Looks like you're going back a long way," Kathryn says wryly, walking over to us and pointedly looking down at our files. "1944, really? You do know that crocodiles can move, right? Where it might have been seven years ago doesn't much matter." She frowns at the page. "Wait, that's not a Crocodile sighting. That's a… survey report…"

"By Ralph Ellis, yes," I say. "Nothing to worry about. Was there anything else, Ms. Zhang?"

"Why do you care about Ralph's survey reports?"

"It's probably just a coincidence. Anyway, if Ralph were concerned, I'm sure he would be down here right now."

"He's busy. Lunch meeting. He told me to come down and, quote, 'get rid of that busybody,' unquote. I thought I would give you a chance to leave quietly before I go directly to management and have you arrested for trespassing." She looks over to Betty. "And you, Betty, I thought better of. You shouldn't be helping this reprobate."

"People are dying, Kathryn," Betty snaps. "I'll help anyone who gets that to stop."

"Ms. Zhang," I say, before things can get more heated, "we'll be out of here very soon. No need to take the time to talk to upper management."

"Good," Kathryn says, turning away. "A pleasure as always, Mr. Stark. Betty."

As the door closes behind her, Betty clenches her fist. "Ooh," she mutters, "I just want to… should we follow her?"

"No, we actually do need to finish here, and confront Ralph Ellis. To shake the murderer loose, we need to cut away the things that are driving this case, and that means convincing Ellis to admit to the find. Once the tension dials down a bit, we can investigate more carefully, but as it stands we're not far from someone else dying." I gather up the files. "You go and find out where that meeting of his is happening, so that we can crash it. I'll pull out the papers that we need, slip the folders back, and join you."

"Sounds good," Betty says, hurrying off.

I spend the next ten minutes copying important files, and then meet Betty outside the survey office. "Is Ralph still upstairs?" I ask.

"No," Betty sighs. "His secretary said that he's out in the lumber yard talking with some loggers. Something to do with a problem load that just arrived." She shakes her head. "Ambushing him while he's with someone who knows about this is one thing, but I don't think it'll help to drag them into this."

"Hmm…" I rub my chin. "Did she mention which ones?"

"I don't think he told her."

"I didn't think he would. How are you at sneaking around?"

"Pretty good," Betty says, eyes narrowed. "Why?"

"Because I don't think that's what's actually happening. If Ellis were meeting with lumberjacks, it would be a short meeting, and would involve whichever surveyor failed to recognize the lumber as a bad batch. But going alone?"

"I don't know, Basil. It sounds a little bit far-fetched."

"It might be, a little bit. On the other hand, we don't have much to lose. Ellis might be annoyed if he catches us, but we can pretend to be looking at lumber, too. Maybe you think the lumber is what's got the Crocodile riled up?"

"You just keep me around for the alibis," Betty complains with a smile.

"But they're such good alibis. Come on, we might hear something interesting."

"Oh, all right. But don't blame me when you get thrown out of here."

"I never blame anyone when I get thrown out of places. I'm a very responsible person."

The lumber yard is a maze, row after row of lumber stacked in an arrangement which I'm sure made sense to the people doing it. Wood meant for shipping away, for local construction, higher grade and lower grade pieces, all arranged in massive towers with a mixture of large truck-paths and smaller foot-paths between them. The sound of the machinery is just starting up, and the ground is littered with sawdust, which cushions our footsteps as we lurk about. "How are we supposed to find him?" Betty asks quietly. "This area is huge."

"Look for fresh prints in the dust." I gesture down. "There can't be that many people out here. Then listen for voices."

It only takes us a few minutes to spot what we're looking for – a footprint in a particularly thick patch of dust, leading deeper into the yard. We follow the trail cautiously, and find more prints, gradually leading us towards the northern edge of the lumber yard. I still can't hear any voices, though, which confirms my theory. If this were a normal meeting, they'd be talking at full volume. In fact, from what I saw of Ellis, I would expect a certain amount of shouting in the mix. Whispers, on the other hand, wouldn't carry far.

As we approach one turning, though, there's a sudden crash of cascading lumber. Betty and I duck behind a tower, looking at each other. "What was that?" Betty hisses.

"I don't know," I say, "but it sounds bad. Stay here, I'll check it out."

I slip my pistol from my jacket pocket, creeping around the corner towards the sound. It doesn't seem to have carried far enough to be heard from the offices, and there's a second, smaller crash as I inch forward. I see a whisper of movement out of the corner of my eye and spin, only to find Betty right behind me. "What did I say?" I whisper.

"I don't know. Probably something very dumb. Why do you have a gun?"

"In case I need to shoot something, obviously."

Betty grimaces, but nods. She falls a couple of steps back, but keeps pace with me as I approach the source of the sounds.

As we come around the corner, I wince. A large tower of lumber has collapsed across the way, and another seems to have lost a large part of its structure; it's teetering uncertainly, with long carved logs everywhere. At first glance, it looks like a truck has spun out of control, but of course there's no truck present. More worrying, however, is the fact that I can see what looks like a leg sticking out from between two logs, bent and bloody.

"God damn it," I mutter, looking around.

"What happened?" Betty asks, eyes wide. "It looks like…"

"Like a giant monster went on a very brief rampage." I creep towards the pile. "Shout if you see it."

It takes me a minute to shift the logs enough to get a better look at the victim without inadvertently crushing him, but once I do I stop with a sigh. It doesn't matter how fast we work now. Ralph Ellis isn't going to be walking away from this one. He's staring up at the sky, a faint look of shock on his face. His spectacles are lying on the ground beside him, under several heavy logs, and there's a handful of torn scraps of paper in one clenched fist. I frown at the scene, shaking my head.

"Who is it? Is he alright?"

I wave Betty back. "You don't want to see this, trust me. And no. It's Ralph Ellis, and he's dead." I kneel by the body, looking over it, and carefully work the top paper free. I study it, and then slip it back into place. "He's been dead for a while. At least half an hour, I would say. I expect it happened nearly as soon as he got out here."

"Another Crocodile victim?" Betty is looking around nervously. "Do you hear ticking?"

"It wasn't the Crocodile," I say, standing again and peering at the ground. "No tracks. Just a lot of scuffed-up footprints."

Betty swallows. "So whoever asked him to come here for that meeting…"

"Killed him, yes, that would be my guess. Before the lumber came down, though. Look, there's no water on most of these logs. It hasn't rained since they came down, but Ellis's body is wet. He was killed before the most recent shower."

"They lured him out here, killed him, and then started collapsing lumber stacks on him?"

"Exactly," I say softly, following the trail in the dust. "In order to make it look as though a monster had come through. Either the plan was to prepare several towers, and then collapse them in quick succession, but Ellis arrived early, or else the plan to cover this up as a

Crocodile attack was a spur-of-the-moment decision, after the killer murdered Ellis in a moment of passion." I consider. "Probably the latter, honestly, although I'll bet they were considering it."

"But… that second crash only happened a few moments before we arrived," Betty points out, sticking close to me. "Which means…"

I nod, peering around a corner. "They're still here. Hiding, hoping that we'll leave and they can slip away in the confusion."

I look at the nearest tower. There are logs lying on the ground near it, and it seems to be tottering slightly in the wind. Not enough to be at a serious risk of falling, but I expect it was the next target. I creep forwards, spotting a dark shadow on the ground across the way. It looks like our mysterious killer is crouching down. I press myself tight against the pile of timbers they're using for cover, raise my pistol, and slowly creep towards them.

"Look out!"

Betty, racing up from behind, grabs me by the coat with a terrific yank. I follow her lead, leaping back towards her, which saves the both of us. As it turns out, my hunch was wrong; the lumber stack I was aiming for wasn't meant to be the third to collapse. It was meant to be the fourth.

The stack of lumber directly next to us gives way in a rush as the shadow moves, raining heavy logs down on top of us. Since I'm already in motion I just keep going, and Betty and I grab each other as we roll out of the cascading wood. One log lands across my leg, and I let out a grunt of pain as I feel something give. Another strikes a glancing blow across my side, and a third bounces across my upper arm. For several seconds the cascade continues, and I cover my head and do my best to shield Betty from the worst of it, only to realize that she's already doing her best to shield me. I can't help but laugh.

"Still there?" I ask, as the dust begins to settle.

"I'm alive," Betty groans, through gritted teeth. "Took a couple of glancing hits, and I think my wrist is sprained, but basically I'm alright."

"Good," I groan. "Do you think you can stand?"

"I told you, I'm fine."

"Could you help me get this log off, then? I'm not sure I have the leverage."

Betty wriggles out from under me, stands up, and grabs the log in question, lifting it with a grunt of effort. I quickly slide my leg to safety, wincing as I stand and test it. Bruised, battered, possibly sprained, but it doesn't seem broken. I look around, spot my pistol on the ground, and scoop it up. The casing is battered, and I'm not sure how well it will fire, but it's better than nothing. "Damn it," I mutter. "That was close. Thank you for the warning."

"No problem," Betty says with a shaky laugh. "Just paying you back."

"Well, I'll keep it in – down!" This time, it's me yanking on her, diving to the ground as a gunshot sounds and a bullet slices through the air above us. I raise my pistol to return fire, but our assailant is already running. "Stay with Ellis!" I bark, rising back to my feet.

Betty, lying on her back, looks up at me incredulously. "What are you doing?"

"Going after a murderer," I snarl, breaking into a sprint. I hear Betty yell for me to wait, but I'm already around the corner, eyes peeled for any more towers. I don't expect there to be any. This has all the hallmarks of a last-minute plan, and I expect that the killer hasn't had time to prepare too many to fall. A panic-stricken attempt to take us out seems more likely than a cool, collected plan, not the least because if he'd waited a few more seconds I would probably be dead, and possibly Betty, too.

I come around a corner, see someone duck around the corner ahead of me, and yell, "Stop!" The rain has started again, slowly turning the damp dust to mud under our feet, and I grit my teeth against a new blossom of pain from my injured leg and push on, after them. As I reach the corner, a shot rings out, and I duck back behind cover. I risk a quick look and another shot slams into a stack of lumber across the way. My quarry is a good ways down the row, now, a grey coat turned up and a black hat pulled down low, far enough away that I can't make out many details. They take another shot at me, but their aim is terrible, and it smashes into the side of my cover without coming close to hitting me.

As soon as they fire, I step out into the lane, raising my pistol and squeezing the trigger. I feel it jam, the body kicking as the bullet fails to fire, and I throw it aside with a curse. I start to run after the killer, but I feel something give way in my leg, and I stumble from the surge of pain that rushes through my body. By the time my vision clears and I'm stumbling forward again, I can see a Jeep racing away into the woods, through open gates.

I stagger up to the gate, seeing a guard running towards me. "Who was that?" I shout.

"What the hell happened to you, man?" The guard stares at me. "You look like you went through a blender!"

"Did you see who was in that car?" I repeat. The guard is looking me up and down, and frowning.

"No, I didn't see who was in that car," he says. "I heard a shot and came running over, and I found… you…" His frown deepens. "Who the hell are you, anyway?"

"Look, would you just go after that damned car?" I yell. "There is a murderer in it, and I don't have a car of my own!"

"A murderer?!" The guard gapes. "Someone's been killed?"

"God damn it!" The Jeep is long gone now; no chance of following it. I let out a long breath, and sag against the nearest tower of logs. "Forget it. Just go ahead and call the police. And perhaps get a doctor out here."

"Basil!" Betty is staggering out of the tower nearby. "Did you get him?"

"Ms. Wescoff? What…" The guard starts. Betty rounds on him.

"Damn it, Geoff, call the police! And a doctor!"

The guard finally listens, racing off, and Betty sinks down next to me. "I honestly don't know how you get through investigations most of the time."

"I thought I said to stay with Ellis."

"I don't recall being your employee."

I breathe out slowly. "They had a gun."

"They were a terrible shot, though. Anyway, you had a gun, too, and a limp to go with it. I figured I had a good chance of catching up, and helping you if you got shot or something." She sighs. "Poor Ralph. I know that he was a criminal, and he may have gotten people killed by mistake, but… he didn't deserve to die for it. Who do you think killed him? One of his bosses?"

"No, that would have been a clean kill. This was a goddamn mess." I shake my head. "The killer was the same person who's been hounding Driscoll, the same person who killed Acker. Someone furious when he found out that Acker had been stealing, and just as furious to find the same thing out about Ralph. Emotional, quick to explode but just as quick to regain his cool." I shake my head. "Jake Collins."

"Are you sure it was him?"

"Absolutely. Ellis had a stack of papers in his hands, which someone tried to tear out of them – balance sheets. Someone finally noticed that he was skimming, and probably also that the company was part of the deal. He killed Ellis by mistake, and then started sabotaging the towers to cover his tracks."

"That doesn't explain why it was Jake. It could have been Kathryn or Andrew."

"Only Jake would display this blend of cunning and idiocy. It's the same pattern of behaviour he showed when we were speaking. He kept almost exploding and then dialing it back. Kathryn Zhang was cool, collected, even when she was angry with me. She never lost control, and I don't think she would be too upset about a few missing pieces as long as she got her cut. Her big concern was keeping things quiet. If she were going to put together a murder, she would have tried to frame Ellis for killing Acker, close things up.

"As for Andrew, if he were guilty he might have faked the Crocodile in his yard, but the level of investigation was already perfect for a cover-up. Bringing me in to look into things ensured that the whole case would be busted open, one way or the other. For an innocent party more afraid of death than jail, it makes sense. For anyone else, it would have been raw idiocy." I shake my head. "No, I'm almost certain Collins is the killer, of both Acker and Ellis. When the Crocodile ate Thatch, it gave him the idea to cover the deaths with a fake Crocodile, and he went after Driscoll too because he couldn't leave well enough alone."

Betty whistles. "We need to warn the others."

I nod. "We absolutely do. How about you do that. I'll wait here for doctors to arrive."

"Sure, get me to do all the hard work." Betty smiles. "Are you going to be alright on your own?"

"I always have been up to now," I say. "Go on. Get to Driscoll and Zhang before Collins decides to come back to get rid of witnesses." Betty nods, and starts away. I stay where I am, and close my eyes. I figure I've earned a bit of a rest. Just for a few minutes.

I'm still there when the police arrive, about twenty minutes later, an ambulance in tow. The fact that the doctor pronounces me fit to walk, after a bit of poking around, surprises me more than a little. The fact that the officer on duty immediately arrests me as a potential murderer doesn't.

I'm dragged to a side room and put under police watch while the boys in blue start looking around. It's not long before an officer walks in accompanied by Betty, who sports a large bandage on her forehead and has her left arm in a sling. She is unceremoniously sat down, with her good arm handcuffed to the table, and then the officer steps back and sits down. "What happened to you?" I ask, brow furrowed.

"Well, it's a long story," she says slowly, glancing at the police officer.

"I think we have a few minutes."

"It started when I got back to where Ralph… to where he died." Betty shakes her head. "I asked the officers where you'd gone, and they wanted to know why I cared. So I told them we were working together, and they told me they thought you were a criminal. Then things got a little… heated."

"Please tell me you didn't take a swing at anyone," I sigh.

"She came damned close," comes the voice from the door. Betty and I look over, to find several of Everland's Finest standing in the doorway. At their forefront is a woman about my age, black hair framing her grim expression, arms crossed over her uniform. She gives me a long look. "You've looked better."

"Hazards of the trade," I say. "Betty Wescoff, allow me to introduce Detective Ellen Gardener, of the Everland Police Department. Detective Gardener is one of the more diligent officers of the North Precinct."

"Rare to hear such kind words from you."

"She's also marginally less corrupt than her compatriots," I add.

"That's more like what I expected," Gardener says. She steps into the room, looking at the two of us. "What are you up to this time, Stark? We caught your friend trying to sneak out the back way, we've got a dead man in a lumber yard that looks like a tornado hit it, we've got Crocodile sightings all through the forest and," she reaches into her jacket and pulls out a sheaf of papers, "there's the matter of these classified documents you were carrying."

"Alright, I can explain those," I say.

"Can you."

"Well… no, not really. But I'm confident that I won't be prosecuted for them once we work out an immunity deal."

Detective Gardener's eyebrows rise so high they vanish into her hair. "You think you have something worth that?"

"Keep hold of those, and we both will." I turn to Betty. "You didn't reach Zhang and Driscoll?"

"They weren't in the office, and these cops grabbed me before I could check anywhere else. Jacob must have told them I was with you."

"Once again, the police and security pay out rich dividends of usefulness." I groan, and rub my forehead. It takes a moment, what with the handcuffs, but I need to think. "Detective Gardener, we need to move quickly. There could be people in serious danger."

"Really," Gardner says dryly. "There always seem to be people in serious danger when we meet, Stark. Funny how that works out." She snaps her fingers, and an officer steps up. "But I'll bite. Give me the names and descriptions of these people, and let me know where to find them."

"Kathryn Zhang, and Andrew Driscoll." I spend a few moments going over the descriptions. "Hopefully, they're still on site. If not, you may need to dispatch officers to their homes. Now that he's been backed into a corner, Collins is going to be dangerous."

Gardener sits down across from us, as her men go to find the others. "Bearing in mind that I am still just humouring you, I suggest that you tell me the whole thing."

"You aren't going to like the whole thing. Who are you taking more bribes from right now, incidentally – Hawthorne, or Second Star?"

Gardener's jaw clenches. "I don't take bribes."

"Gifts, then. Whatever you feel like calling them. The point is, if I tell you everything, you're going to have to make a choice."

"Stark…"

"Alright, your funeral." It's not my habit to work with cops from the North Precinct, but if I have to, at least I can trust that Gardener isn't going to drag us into a back alley and shoot us. She might even owe me when this is done. I give Gardener an only slightly edited version of events, in which the responsibility for the site falls on Ralph Ellis. In my version, the surveyors were pressured into their fraudulent activities by threats and blackmail held over their heads to force cooperation. Driscoll brought me in to investigate, not the Crocodile, but Ellis himself, hoping to find a way to win free of the activities that he's found himself a part of. I'm not sure if Gardener buys it, but I'm also not sure if it matters, because as I show her the evidence of the claims that Ellis forged in the past, I can see the gears turning in her head.

"You're right, Stark," she says when I'm done. "I don't like this."

"Warned you."

"You realize the damage that this could do to Hawthorne Logging if it came out. We're talking about corporate fraud on a vast scale. Second Star wouldn't let it slide."

"They would not."

"And I'm going to have to tell them anyway, aren't I."

"I expect so. At the very least, we need to warn people about the corollary between moving celestial graveyards, and Crocodile attacks."

Gardener groans. "I assume you're going to want to corroborate all of this," she mutters to Betty, who nods sweetly. "Of course," Gardener says. "Well, I didn't much like being a cop anyway."

"Oh, don't think of it like that, Gardener. After all, when all this comes to light, Second Star is going to owe you big. Maybe you can get a transfer to the DA's office."

"And I suppose you'll talk to your connections to make that happen," Gardener says sourly.

"I'm sorry, I thought that you **didn't** want to be fired."

"Fair enough." Gardener stands. "I don't like this, Stark, but I'm inclined to agree with you. I assume that immunity is going to be your condition for actually swearing to any of this? Because if I get into court and you back out on me, I will go down in flames."

"Immunity for myself, Betty, and Andrew Driscoll. The case couldn't have been solved without them."

"No guarantees. But I think it'll work out."

"Of course it will. The Old Man has every prosecutor in the city in his Rolodex, and you know he'll be furious when he finds out about this. The chance to pin

Hawthorne's board to the wall is going to be too good to pass up." I shake my head. "But Ellis is dead. I think I can guarantee that Driscoll will talk, but if you can grab Collins, it would really shore up your case."

This is the point where one of Gardener's cops rushes back in. "Ma'am," he says, saluting. "We found Ms. Zhang, and she's in protective custody right now. She's refusing to admit to any involvement, and demanding to be allowed to call her lawyer. But there's no sign of Andrew Driscoll. We checked the register, and he seems to have checked out a Jeep fifteen minutes ago."

"That can't be right," I say. "That was after all of the chaos started."

"Are you still sure it was Collins who killed Ellis?" Gardener asks. "Maybe Driscoll got tired of waiting for you."

"Not his style," I say. "I can't imagine why…" I break off. "Collins. He must have grabbed Driscoll and faked his signature."

"For what possible reason?"

"He needs to move the starstone, and fast. If he can make it look like this was all Driscoll's idea, he can use him to load the stone up, and then leave him in the woods and drive for town. Driscoll might claim otherwise, but Collins can't know that we're on to him. Driscoll takes the fall, and Collins gets away with the goods."

"Unless Andrew's already dead," Betty says, looking worried. "I mean, a dead witness can't tell tales."

"I don't think so," I say, shaking my head. "He'll want to gather the stone, and then fake a crash or something on the way back to town. It's that blend of stupid and clever I was telling you about. No, I'll bet you that if we can get to wherever Ellis stashed the stone, we'll find Collins and Driscoll there." I look over to Gardener. "We need to speak with Ms. Zhang immediately."

"She's already lawyered-up," Gardener points out.

"Then," I say, standing up, "it's a good thing that I'm not the police."

Kathryn Zhang is being held, ironically, in the same supply area that we used for our conversation the day before, sitting on the one chair in the room, hands cuffed behind her back. The police reluctantly let me in, once again free of handcuffs, and even more reluctantly close the door behind me, leaving me alone in the room with her.

Kathryn looks up at me, frowning. "Well, well," she says. "I suppose you think you're very clever."

"I do, rather," I admit. "Although in this case, I think you might want to do something clever yourself. I'm sure you heard when you were being rounded up. Ralph Ellis is dead."

"I heard," Kathryn says, looking down. For a moment, I think her lip is trembling, but when she looks back up her eyes are hard. "I don't see what it has to do with me. I didn't kill him."

"Come off it, Kathryn," I say. "There are no police in here. Just the two of us. Collins killed Sam Acker. He killed Ralph Ellis, and if we can't catch him, he is going to kill Andrew Driscoll."

"So why are you talking to me?"

"Because I don't know where he is!" I snarl. "He's gone to your cache, I assume. To gather up the starstone, or as much of it as he can carry. He's probably making Driscoll do most of the heavy lifting. But when he's done, he won't have any need for Driscoll any more, and he is clearly a man used to violence." I look at her. "You're right. You didn't kill Acker, or Ellis. But if you don't tell me where the hell I'm supposed to go now, you are going to kill Driscoll."

Kathryn winces. "There's a cave in Grid H-11," she says. "It's in the area where Jim Thatch died. Northwest corner of the grid, blocked off and marked as an unstable underground location, to keep people away."

"You hid the starstone in the middle of an active logging operation?"

"Loggers don't go into caves, even in hilly areas. The stuff was concealed, and having active logging meant that we could drive Jeeps in and out of the area without anyone getting suspicious. It seemed like a foolproof plan, until Thatch was killed and the police started looking around the area. Once that happened, we didn't have a chance to go in and move anything. All of the starstone should still be there." Kathryn looks at me. "If the police ask, of course, that's just an educated guess."

"Still trying to cover yourself?"

"Someone has to. We can't all afford private eyes to look out for us." She waves as best she can. "Go and save Andrew. He's a pillock, but he's a nice enough guy. Wouldn't want to see him hurt."

I go outside, and meet up with Gardener. "You get anything?"

"She gave an 'educated guess'. We need to grab the survey maps – the cave we're looking for is in the northwest corner of Grid H-11."

"Sounds like your work here is done, then," Gardener says.

"Sounds like," I agree. "I suppose you'll be escorting me back to my makeshift cell."

"I would never do that to you. I'll be escorting you to a squad car, so that we can take you to a proper cell."

"My mistake."

"Just between you and me, though," Gardener says, as she starts to walk me down the corridor, "I think you'll get your deal. I've placed a few calls to the precinct, and people are very interested in your story."

She hands me off to a pair of officers and goes to hunt down the survey maps, and I follow meekly along. Betty is waiting in the squad car, and she nods to me as I'm gently, but firmly, placed into the back seat. "Well, you did warn me," she says. "Are they going to get him?"

"I certainly hope so. They have everything that they need."

"Good. And are we going to jail forever?"

"Probably not. A few days, I would guess."

"Even better." Betty sighs, leaning back against the seat. "I would have liked to see how it was going to end."

"Let me spoil it for you – there'll be violence, Collins will be arrested, Driscoll will probably be fine, and so will we. You'll have plenty of time at the trial to hear about the rest." I frown, looking out the window. Gardener has returned, and is talking intently with the police officers who were about to get into the car. "Now, that's odd," I murmur.

Betty follows my look. "What's going on out there?"

"I think we might be about to find out. Good afternoon, detective. I didn't expect to see you so soon."

"Out of the car," Gardener says, jerking her thumb. I obey, and am surprised to find my and Betty's handcuffs being removed.

"Not that I'm upset, but what's all this about?"

"Hawthorne are dragging their heels," Gardener says sourly. "They've called up an injunction preventing us from poking around the woods until the Regulators arrive."

"And how long will that be?"

"Apparently, about two hours. There's a hot tip about the Crocodile that the local teams have rushed off to investigate, and they can't be reached."

"That doesn't sound right."

"I agree. I told them that someone's life could be in danger, and they threatened to treat us as trespassers if we try to enter a restricted area."

"What?" Betty looks between us, incredulous. "Why?"

"They want Collins to escape," I explain grimly. "If he can take the starstone away, and Driscoll with him, the case against Hawthorne gets a lot weaker."

"You might also be interested to know that they confiscated those papers we found on you," Gardener says. "Apparently you had every right to them, and we were wrong to consider them evidence."

I slowly smile. "So they aren't pressing charges."

"They are not. And under the circumstances, I don't consider you a credible suspect. You understand, I'm sure." Gardener nods to me. "Go home, Stark. We'll let you know how it goes. Come on, men." She turns and strides away, two confused officers following in her wake. I tap Betty on the arm.

"Are you still interested in seeing how this ends?"

"…Yes."

"Even if it might, just possibly, end with us being eaten by a Crocodile, or shot by a murderer?"

"I think you may have lost me."

"Gardener's giving us free reign to go after Collins," I say, as I start towards the motor pool. "She's using the fact that Hawthorne are being obstreperous to let us go, and not posting anyone to follow us to make sure we go in the right direction. She and her men are going to run interference so that Hawthorne's security folk don't realize that we've gone. They'll be behind us, but not until they realize what's going on."

"So we might get shot."

"Oh, by any number of people." I shrug. "You don't have to come along, of course. I used to be quite good at exploring these woods, back in the day. It would help to have someone who knows what the terrain looks like now, though." I pause. "Also, I can't drive."

Betty gestures to her sling. "I'm not going to be winning any races today either."

"No, I mean at all. Never learned. Can you handle a Jeep one-handed?"

She frowns, dubiously. "Maybe. If we don't move too fast."

"Better than nothing. Come on. Let's steal a car and get moving – maybe we'll be lucky and spot a friendly lumberjack along the way, but we can't count on that. We have a life to save."

After a brief trip upstairs to steal the surveying map, we find an unattended Jeep at the motor pool, and start to climb in. As we do, a guard marches over to us. "Hey!" he shouts. "You aren't signed off for that!"

Betty gives him a broad smile. "I'm just finishing off my investigation," she says sweetly. "Didn't the paperwork come through?"

"No, it didn't," the man says suspiciously. "I heard you were talking to the police?"

"Just a few routine questions."

"I don't know about this…"

"Oh, for the love of God, I don't have time for this!" The guard blinks, and Betty quickly recovers. "I mean,

I've got about two hours' drive each way, and I am not good at night driving. I really have to get moving now."

"But…"

Betty and I share a look, and she turns the key in the ignition. She gives the guard her brightest smile. "Thanks! Just sign my name into the book, it'll be fine."

"But…"

The Jeep guns out of the lot and through the open gate, leaving the guard staring blankly and still trying to marshal a defence. I clap slowly. "Couldn't have done it better myself," I say. "I'm beginning to think that I'm a bad influence."

"Just now, you think that? Before I met you, I'd never even shoplifted, and in the last two days I've been menaced by thugs, hopped a taxi with a near-stranger, broken into a locker room, lied to my bosses, witnessed a murder, was almost crushed to death by fallen logs, got shot at, and now I've stolen a car."

"And…?"

"And I'm loving every minute of it," Betty says. "Well, aside from poor Ralph. But yes, you are absolutely a terrible influence."

"Glad to hear it."

"Which way are we going?"

I spend a few moments consulting the map. "The north road for the moment. We'll curve west, past the logging camp, and then north again for about eight miles. Shouldn't take too long."

"Alright. Keep the directions coming," Betty says, gunning the engine. "And keep an eye out for giant crocodiles."

The Jeep takes us deep into the woods, but aside from one tight moment when it looks like we're stuck in a mud patch, we don't have any trouble. As we start to approach the hideout, I lean over to Betty. "Alright, cut the engine. I'll take over from here."

Betty pulls the Jeep up to a tree, and then turns it off. "Do you have a plan?"

"I always have a plan."

"Great. What is it?"

"Sneak into the cave, see what's happening, and then find a way to stop Collins based on what I see. It's a very adaptable plan."

"Lovely. Do you have a weapon?"

"Well, not as such."

"So your plan is literally to just hope for the best."

"I'll be fine. Stay with the Jeep in case we need to make a quick getaway, please."

"Fine. But only because my arm feels sore from the driving." Betty glares at me. "Be careful."

"Promise."

I slip out of the car, and start across the muddy terrain. It reminds me of old times, hunting with the Piccadilly, although a nagging voice at the back of my mind reminds me that I was never more than a passable hunter, and that my best years are behind me. Also that my leg is still aching, I've got a headache threatening to erupt, and it's mostly willpower keeping me going.

I could really use a drink.

In absence of that, I settle for imagining all of the things that I would have done to Collins in my pirate days, as I slip through the underbrush. I've deliberately parked us a good five-minute walk from the cave, in order to have the best chance of slipping up on him, so I have plenty of time as I watch for fallen twigs or bushes likely to tear. In this sense, the rain – which is just starting up again – is a godsend. The sound conceals my footsteps, and the wet earth swallows what little sound I would otherwise have made. As I climb the steep hill, picking my way between the trees, I keep an ear out, but don't hear anything at all. The woods are ominously still, either frightened by the rain or by our Jeep.

Out of the corner of my eye, I spot a metallic sheen through the trees, and angle myself towards it. Another Jeep, half-covered with a net, but clearly taken from the Hawthorne camp, is sitting on a rocky outcropping, near a narrow cave mouth. I creep up the hill, and crouch down beside it. The engine is still warm, and the top has been left down; the interior is slowly being soaked. In the back are four small, but heavy-looking, crates, with plenty of room for more.

I make my way towards the cave mouth, listening intently, and sure enough I soon hear grunts of effort slowly approaching. I quickly duck behind several bushes, throwing myself into the mud, as Jake Collins emerges from the cave mouth, pistol in hand, and looks around suspiciously. He's not looking well; his suit is covered in mud, his hair is plastered to the side of his face, and there are scratches on his hands, along with old blood drying on his forehead. It looks like someone got a few hits in. His gun, on the other hand, is pristine, and the way he flicks it around suggests that he'll fire at the slightest provocation.

After a few moments, Jake apparently decides that the coast is clear. He vanishes for a moment, and then returns hefting a large crate in his hands. I debate jumping him, but I don't have a good way to sneak up on the man, and if he sees me coming he's liable to double back into the cave and use Driscoll as a hostage. Instead I wait for him to be occupied levering the crate onto the back of his Jeep, a process made slower by his unwillingness to let go of his pistol, and then creep into the cave itself. Busy as he is, Jake doesn't notice a thing, and I'm able to get inside without difficulty.

The interior of the cave is a short, narrow tunnel, no more than three feet wide, which curves around some rocks and opens into a large space. The rock wall here has been expanded, and wooden struts prop it up, but it's largely a natural space that feels more than a little claustrophobic. I can see a thin trickle of water running along the ground, from cracks in the walls and ceiling, and the dark room is lit by a couple of gas lamps sitting in the corner, which can't be good for the air quality. There are about twenty crates stacked against one wall, and large pieces of ore are piled up next to them; in the dim light, they give off a faint, golden shimmer.

Sitting next to the boxes, with his ankles locked together by handcuffs, is Andrew Driscoll, loading starstone into one of the crates. He looks tired, his suit is covered in mud and his hair is plastered to his face, but he doesn't seem hurt. As he looks up, I quickly put my finger over my lips, and his almost-shout is choked off. I cross over to him and kneel, looking at the handcuffs. "Are you alright?" I ask.

"He's completely lost it," Driscoll says faintly. "He's been ranting. Said that Ellis was trying to cheat us, that Sam was trying to cheat us. Blamed me for ruining everything when he wasn't blaming them."

I nod, pulling out a pair of picks and working on the cuffs. "I suspected as much. I'm glad you aren't hurt."

"I've been mostly just agreeing with him. It seemed safer."

"Smart man. We'll get these off you, jump him when he comes back in, and turn him over to the police. No problem."

"Oh, I think there'll be a problem, Mr. Stark." I wince, and stand slowly. It looks like Collins is quieter than I gave him credit for. He's standing by the cave mouth, his pistol pointing straight at me. "Step away from Andrew, please."

I do so, turning around. "Mr. Collins," I say politely. "Fancy running into you here. You might as well put the gun away."

"And why would I possibly do that?"

"You don't think I came alone, do you?" I laugh. "The police know where you are, Collins. They know what's going on. I just snuck in ahead of them to try and get Mr. Driscoll out, in the hopes that it would convince you to stand down. If you give yourself up, it will go better for you. What do you say?"

"I say you're a liar, and a cheat," Collins snarls. "This is all your fault! I know what you're up to, Stark. You're just trying to steal all of this." His gun waves wildly at the starstone. "Your story about the Crocodile! It's all just a lie, to try and scare us off, so that you can split the find with Andrew! It's your idea, to cheat us out of our rightful shares. Well, it's not going to work, you hear me! I'm   not   afraid!"

"Scare you off? I'm not the one killing his partners."

"They were trying to cheat us!" Collins yells. "Andrew knows. He understands. Sam was stealing starstone, using it to pay off his damned gambling debts. The idiot started betting more, just because he knew there was a payday coming, and he blew through it all so fast…" He breaks off shaking his head. "I didn't mean to kill him," he says. "It was just an accident."

"You asked him to come out to the woods because you'd found out about the shortages, I expect. The two of you were friends, weren't you?"

"We fought. I knew he was gambling, I just didn't know… it wasn't my fault. He was just so snide. Said it didn't matter, it would all just be made up with the next load. As if the rules didn't apply to him. He always thought…" Collins breaks off again. "I hit him. Maybe I hit him harder than I should have. It wasn't my fault."

"And then you panicked. You had a dead body, in the woods, and then it came to you… the Crocodile. You weren't far from where Thatch died. You could fake up the body, and no one would wonder about it because they would be too busy covering it up."

"Might as well use company greed for me, for a change," Collins agrees. "I wasn't going to lose everything just because Sam was an idiot. It was his fault, anyway, Stark!"

"And was Ralph his own fault?" I ask, taking a small step forward.

"No, that was yours!" Collins points the gun back at me. I'm starting to regret needling him. "Poking around, asking questions. Stirring things up that should have stayed buried. You made me start looking too, so that there wouldn't be records that proved we were involved. And then I found out how much Sam was making with his starstone sales. More than Ralph had said, a lot more. And I found out about the other finds, and I realized how much he was cheating us. I took the papers to confront him, and he attacked me."

"Ridiculous."

"Excuse me?" Collins raises his gun and steps towards me.

"I said that's ridiculous!" I snap. "You knew exactly what you were doing when you lured him out there, where no one would find him. You couldn't sabotage those lumber piles by hand. You needed an ax, and pliers, to snap the chains holding them tight and weaken key pillars. You were already planning to kill him when you met him."

"No! I wasn't!" Collins almost sobs, waving the gun again. "It was just… I needed to be ready. In case he attacked me. I knew he would."

"You're a paranoid wreck," I say with a sigh. "It probably started as soon as you found the starstone. Ellis should never have brought you onboard. You just weren't cut out for this. Did you start to panic right away, or did you wait until Thatch died? Did you think he was after the starstone, too?" I shake my head. "Give me the gun, Collins. What kind of life is it going to be, trying to run from the police? Even if you somehow get out of here alive, they will always be on your tail, always right behind you. Anyone could be an informer. Anyone could be a threat." I lock eyes with him. "Anyone could be lurking, ready to take you out. You'll never have a moment's peace."

Collins raises the gun. "Maybe not, but I'm not going to prison because someone else cheated me. Goodbye, Mr. Stark."

The stone flinging through the air catches him on the shoulder, and he yells with fright and spins. As he does I launch myself at him, and the gun goes off as I slam him into the ground. He struggles for a moment, trying to get the pistol in line to remove me, but it only takes a couple of punches to the gut to leave him curled in a ball, and I wrench the pistol out of his hand. "I thought," I say severely to the tunnel mouth, "I told you to stay with the Jeep."

Betty emerges, sheepishly, another stone in her hand. "Oh, yes," she says, "you had everything under control."

"You could have been shot."

"Well, I wasn't much safer outside, and you looked like you could use a hand."

I pause. "What? Why not?"

"We have a problem, is why."

"What kind of problem?"

"The kind that ticks."

I look down the tunnel mouth. Behind me, Driscoll is gaping, caught off-guard by the development, and in the quiet all I can hear is us breathing, and the faint gasps from Collins as he vaguely struggles. And then I hear it, too. Drifting across the air.

Tick. Tock.

"Of course," I mutter. "Nothing is ever easy."

"I heard it in the woods," Betty says. "I gunned the Jeep's engine, and then ran for cover when it came out to fight. Which worked, but had a couple of downsides."

"The Jeep's wrecked?"

"The Jeep is wrecked," Betty says with a nod. "So I am open to ideas."

"Maybe we hide here until the police arrive?" Driscoll suggests. "You said they were right behind you."

"Well… that might have been a slight exaggeration. Certainly, they will arrive. In a few hours. Or maybe a day." I frown at the tunnel. "What do you think? Could a Crocodile get through that? It's fairly narrow, and it is quite a large beast."

"I'm not crawling back to check," Betty says, with a shiver.

"Fine," I say. "Watch Collins, in case he tries to be clever. In fact, wait a moment, I'm going to handcuff him." I finish removing Driscoll's handcuffs and use them on Collins, collect a couple of pieces of starstone and Collins' pistol, and step up to the dark crack in the wall. "No problem," I mutter. I tilt my head, listening carefully.

Tick, Tock.

It is echoing down the tunnel. "I think it's lurking outside," I whisper to the others. "Is there another way out of here?"

"I don't know," Driscoll says. He gestures back into the cave. "We never really checked farther in. It didn't seem safe."

"Oh. Good. That's… very cautious of you." I rub my forehead. "My expense report is going to be a work of art, I can promise you that." I take a deep breath, looking at the tunnel. "Maybe we should just wait here for the police," I say quietly. "At least for an hour or so. Might be safer. For now, let's just be quiet and…"

"This is some kind of trick!" Collins yells. "You're just trying to scare me into confessing! The Crocodile isn't real!"

The ticking, almost immediately, gets louder. It's coming from everywhere, now, echoing through the caves. "Thank you, Collins, for that remarkable insight into a paranoia-filled mind. I don't even… how would we… you know what, never mind. Driscoll, can you walk?"

Driscoll stands shakily, rubbing his legs. He takes a few careful steps. "I think so."

"Good. I'm going to take one of those lamps and see if the monster is right outside. It shouldn't take too long." The ticking is getting maddening. "But I don't think it's going to be right outside."

As it turns out, I am right. The Crocodile is not right outside.

My first hint of this is when its jaws erupt from a crack in the wall to my left, sending sharp splinters of rock in every direction. I dive to the side, barely in time to avoid having my arm bitten off, and crash painfully into a cluster of starstone. Collins screams, falling over as he tries to simultaneously stand, run, and babble something about impossible monsters. Betty grabs Driscoll, who is stumbling, and pulls him to the other side of the cave as the Crocodile's jaws open and snap on the other side. It's trying to force its way through the narrow gap, and the cave walls are trembling from the force. I see a rock come loose from the ceiling and crash to the ground, and wince. "We're going to have to run for it!" I shout. "I'll distract it, you grab Driscoll and Collins and get out!"

"How are you going to distract it?" Betty yells back, pushing Driscoll as close to the exit as she can get without getting in range of the Crocodile. It's gradually taking up more space in the room, which doesn't feel nearly as large as it did a minute ago, and it doesn't seem like it will take long before the monster's entire head has forced its way from the wall. "Shoot it?"

I look down at the pistol. "No, I don't think so." Instead, I heft one of the starstone pieces, and give it a soft, underhand toss towards the Crocodile. It pauses for a moment, sniffing at the stone, and then gives another attempt to snap at me. I circle away from the others, gathering more rocks, and continue tossing them towards the creature. Each time I do, there is a short pause. "Now! Go!"

"What about you?"

"I will be fine! Go!"

Betty nods, and shoves Driscoll through the opening. Collins stumbles through behind her, still staring at the Crocodile's jaws in disbelief, as I keep tossing rocks towards it. Each time, the pause before it tries to force its way through again is shorter, and actually I think it's getting angrier, rather than less angry. It certainly doesn't seem interested in eating these stones.

I give Betty a minute to get through the tunnels, and then consider my options. The problem here is that I don't have any. The Crocodile is furious, and since it's wriggling its way towards me, the path to the tunnel that we slipped in through is mostly gone. I could try to shoot it, but that's just going to make it angry, and the lamps aren't going to do anything.

I've only really got one choice, and with an injured leg I don't like my chances. But it's better than nothing. Carefully, I take off my coat, filling it with starstone. The Crocodile sees the movement and strains to get closer, dragging its body a few more inches through the tight tunnel it created. Its front legs are in the cave now, scrabbling for purchase, and the sound of the clock in its gullet fills the room. I can feel its breath on my cheeks, forcing the air out of the room.

I keep piling starstone into my coat. The Crocodile snarls and lunges again, and I see its body beginning to slip through the cracks; the largest part of it is almost through, which means I'm out of time. With a massive heave, I throw the entire coatfull of stones as hard as I can, bouncing them off the creature's face. For a moment, it looks down at them, and its frenzy goes still. In that instant, I leap as hard as I can, landing on top of its head.

The Crocodile goes berserk. It tries to rear back, and I bounce up, hit the ceiling, and slam back down on top of it. I roll along its back, feeling the scales tearing at my shirt, and land by the tunnel mouth. As the Crocodile tries to shift its body to lunge at me, finally filling the cave as its bulk clears the tunnel, I fire several shots into the support pillars, and one into the oil lamp sitting on the ground. The lamp explodes with a satisfying sound, which doesn't do much more than distract the Crocodile for a moment, but that's really all that I need. I push into the narrow tunnel, moments before the monster's jaws snap shut on the entrance, still too close for comfort.

I scramble down the tunnel as quickly as possible, hearing the angry growl of the Crocodile mixing with the sound of ticking as it tries to force itself into the opening. I can hear its tail smashing against the wall of the cave as it moves, and the cracking sound of stone, and there only seems to be one possible outcome. The support struts, which I did some damage to between the minor fires and the hail of bullets, start to give way, and the already-unstable cave starts to collapse.

I can feel the tunnel walls trembling, and I push through as fast as possible. Standing by the entrance of the cave, Betty reaches in and grabs me, and we half-run, half-tumble from the cave mouth as stones give way, the tunnel vanishing in a cloud of dust and rock fragments. I cough, looking down at what remains of my shirt, and nod to her. "We have to stop meeting like this."

"You are terrible at sincerity," Betty says. She looks past me. "Is it dead?"

"Somehow, I doubt it. But it should be a few hours before it can dig itself free. I suggest we spend those hours getting far, far away from here. Where are the others?"

"Andrew is hiding in the car Jake Collins stole," Betty says dryly. "And Jake's handcuffed to the back seats. He tried to knock me over and run away as soon as we got out of the caves."

"Of course he did," I sigh. "Did you hurt him very badly?"

"I don't think so."

"Admirable restraint," I say, limping towards the car.

"Are you alright? You're bleeding."

"Where?"

"Your back, mostly. A lot of little cuts."

"Never wrestle with crocodiles, they have a knack for getting even." I shake my head. "Come on. We need to get Collins back into custody, and we need to discuss my immunity deal with Andrew. And then… maybe dinner? I go could for some dinner."

"Dinner sounds lovely," Betty agrees. "Andrew," she yells to the car, "you're driving."

Wednesday

Dinner, as it turns out, is cancelled by police procedures. When we return to the lumber yard we are all promptly arrested by Hawthorne security guards, who accuse us of theft, trespassing, violating their sovereign land, and all manner of other offenses. They aren't mollified by our recovery of Jake Collins, or of a few crates of goods that should not have been on Hawthorne land in the first place, and for a few tense moments I think that the crates are going to vanish, along with Collins.

Fortunately, Detective Gardener is already on site, and insists on taking all of us into custody. She also has a nurse look over our wounds, who complains that we've aggravated many minor injuries from earlier in the day and makes Betty and I promise not to do anything else foolish. From there, we are taken directly to the precinct lockup, where I reiterate my desire for an immunity deal for Betty, Driscoll and myself. There are a few tense hours, during which I think the authorities may decide to send me to jail forever just to never have to deal with me again, but ultimately the district attorney agrees to my terms, and the next day, after giving our depositions and promising to remain in town until the day of Collins' trial, we are released on bail.

I call Holly at the office to give her the good news, and we each go home to change before meeting back at Jessie's to celebrate with a proper brunch. As we get our food, I look around the table. Driscoll is poking forlornly at his eggs, although he certainly finished his first cup of coffee quickly. Betty is more enthusiastic; she's hit it off with Holly at some point while I was showering, and is now chatting with her about the case and digging into her steak with gusto. For her part, Holly isn't eating much of anything, but only because she's peppering us with questions every three seconds. I wait for a break in the inquisition, and then smile to the others. "Well, Mr. Driscoll," I say, "it didn't go quite the way that I expected, but it looks like everything worked for for you."

"For me, yes," Driscoll says with a sigh. "Not so much for Ralph. Or Sam."

"It wasn't your fault," I say, patting him on the arm. "You did quite a lot to get this story to come to light, didn't you? It couldn't have been easy to smash up those rose bushes."

There's a long pause, as Holly and Betty break off their conversation and turn to look at me. "I thought Jake Collins did that," Betty finally says.

I shake my head. "No. Collins didn't want to get rid of Mr. Driscoll. Until I arrived on the scene, in fact, he didn't care about him at all." I look over to Driscoll, who is staring fixedly down at his eggs.

Betty frowns. "I don't understand. Andrew, you… faked the Crocodile stalking you?"

"When did you know?" Driscoll asks quietly.

"I suspected almost immediately," I say wryly. "The footprints in the garden were men's, fairly large. Collins had very small feet, and Ellis's weren't much larger. Now, if the Crocodile had actually been there, it might have made sense for your feet to be the only ones present, but when I ran into the damned thing, it became obvious that sneaky, it was not. And the more I learned about the whole scheme, the more obvious it became. Ralph Ellis wouldn't do it. He was invested in you remaining onboard, or his conspiracy might fall apart. Kathryn Zhang wouldn't do it. She was invested in everything staying quiet. Sam Acker was dead, so he was out. And Jake Collins was busy with his own concerns; everything that he did was focused on the woods, to make it seem like a series of accidents were occurring involving the beast. His entire plan was that Hawthorne would help him cover up his murders, because they didn't want them investigated.

"If the Crocodile was actually stalking you, people would investigate why, and the truth would come out. Collins knew that as well as you did, which is both why he wouldn't have done it, and why you would."

Betty gasps. "You wanted the smuggling ring to come to light!"

Driscoll sighs, putting down his fork. "I was a coward," he says. "I didn't know how Sam died, but it was suspicious. I thought that he might have gotten cold feet, and been killed for it, but I couldn't say that. Not without risking being killed myself."

"So you put together a story that might excuse an investigation. Something that your co-conspirators might not believe, but that they wouldn't fault you for getting me involved in," I say. "And you didn't trust me to play along, at first, so you didn't tell me the truth either. Does that about cover it?"

"I'm sorry, Mr. Stark. If I'd just told you everything, Ralph might not have died."

"Maybe. Maybe you would have died instead. Maybe Collins would have gone on a murder spree if he'd thought you were turning against him, too. It's easy to judge with hindsight, but I understand why you did what you did." I pause, taking a sip of tea, and add, "Of course, brunch is on you."

"Of course," Driscoll says with a faint laugh. "It's the least I can do, after everything that you've done for me."

"It really is," I agree.

The four of us finish our lunch, and Holly agrees to take Driscoll back to the office to finalize our expense account. I assume she'll end up putting more on it than I would have thought of, and that Driscoll is feeling guilty and relieved enough to sign it all without complaint, so I leave them to it. "So," I say to Betty, who's finishing up another slice of pie, "what are your plans?"

"I'm not sure," she says. "Half of Hawthorne's board is about to be in jail, and I expect I'm not going to be welcome around the office any more. Maybe I'll apply to work at Second Star. They can always use engineers. Less fresh air than I've gotten used to, but it might be fun." She chuckles. "Hopefully, it'll be a little bit less adventurous. Are all of your cases this bad?"

"Very few of them, honestly. Mostly it's divorce cases, the occasional mob war. You know, simple things."

"It was sure a hell of a case. I thought I was going to die, oh, three or four times, I think."

"Sorry for dragging you into it."

"Don't be. I don't think I would want to make a habit of it, but it was exciting. And we really made a difference, didn't we?"

"That we did, Betty."

"There's just one thing I don't understand. What did the Crocodile want with the starstone?"

"It was protecting it," I say, finishing my drink.

"What?"

"It never appeared until a graveyard was disturbed. It went after people moving starstone, tried to get the starstone away from us. It didn't do it the way that you and I might, because while it's a clever beast, it's still a beast, but it was protecting the graveyards from us. Trying to keep those fallen stars safe, poor thing."

"Why?"

"I don't know," I say, standing and offering her my hand. "I think, in its own strange, reptilian way, it cared for them. Maybe it simply didn't know that they were dead, and was guarding them while they slept, or maybe, in the end, it just felt that they deserved to have a peaceful rest. We'll probably never know for certain."

"And the mountain?" Betty ignores my hand and stands up herself.

"Well, it'll be off-limits for a long time. If they ever try to excavate it, I expect that they'll find the Crocodile, and the starstone, gone to wherever it hides the pieces it finds. Some other quiet graveyard, where they can rest. And honestly, I say leave them to it. One last hidden corner of peace in the world."

"Why Basil," Betty says, taking my hand as we walk to the door. "I didn't know you had the soul of a poet."

"I've been many things in my life," I say, stepping out in the Everland sun. "If there's one thing I've learned, it's that life is poetic." I turn to look at her. "Shall we go?"

We walk out of the diner, into another fine Everland day.

About the Author

Misha Handman lives in Toronto, Ontario. When not writing fantastical stories, he spends his time working in the arts. He can be found in various places on the internet under the web handle 'Friv Yeti', and is always up to chat with fellow fantasy and mystery enthusiasts.